Secrets Revealed

Charmanie
Saquea

Prologue

Click, Clack

The house got quiet at the sound of a gun cocking. Neicey had that same possessed look on her face that she had when Mykell had slapped her. Mykell just looked at her wondering where she had gotten a gun from while raising his hands in the air.

"Oh no, don't get quiet now bitch. You sho had a lot to say a minute ago. Gon' on ahead and finish what you were saying. I got raped because of what bitch?" She pointed the gun at Mykell. "And you nigga, you're up here pillow talking and discussing me with this bitch? What type of shit is that? I never would have thought that you would be a bitch nigga!"

"Baby, look, it ain't even like that, I never talked about you to this bitch. She's just doing that to fuck with you."

"Oh really? You expect me to believe that? Then how the fuck did she know I was raped then? That shit damn sure wasn't a national headline!"

"Because while you were too stuck on stupid to do anything, he was with me every night," Kya said with a smug look.

All of a sudden, Neicey started praying while moving the gun from Kya to Mykell, back and forth, still looking possessed.

Lord, please forgive me for what I'm about to do. You know my struggle and you know my feelings. Don't charge it to my head and don't charge it to my heart. Charge it to the game.

She aimed the gun at her target and pulled the trigger.

POW!

Chapter 1

Reneice

After I shot that bitch Kya, I turned the gun on Mykell. That nigga was looking like a deer caught in headlights. Kya was on the floor screaming, acting like I did some real damage. I was getting pissed off.

"Shut up bitch! Ain't shit wrong with you, it's just a flesh wound." I turned my attention back to Mykell. "I loved you with all my heart but that still wasn't good enough for you, huh? You wanted this triflin' bitch, well you can have her. Ain't neither one of you dumb birds worth sitting on a double murder charge. Don't call me for shit. As a matter of fact, lose my number. My baby will call and know another nigga as its daddy."

With that said, I put my boyfriend back in my purse and walked out the front door, never looking back. When I got in the car, I broke down. The tears just started flowing non-stop. I called the first person I could think of.

"Hello?"

I couldn't stop crying. "I need you," was all I could get out.

"Use yo key." That was all I needed to hear.

* * *

I opened the door and he was waiting for me. He hugged me and wiped my tears away, like always. That was why I loved him. He was so gentle and caring.

"What happened?"

"I just snapped Mil Mil. I didn't mean to shoot her, but she was making fun about me getting raped and I just lost it," I said in one big breath.

I didn't even know why I chose to go there of all places, seeing as how it was his cousin that I just shot, but that was where I needed to be.

"Whoa, whoa slow down. You shot who?" he asked concerned.

I put my head down and looked at the floor before answering. "Your cousin Kya. I shot your cousin."

He lifted my head up. "Is she dead?" he asked dryly, catching me off guard and making me lose my train of thought.

"Uhh, no. I just gave her a flesh wound."

"Then you have nothing to worry about."

The ringing of my phone paused our conversation momentarily. I looked at the screen and saw Ramone's name. I hit ignore and powered my phone off.

"You're not going to turn me over to the police are you? For shooting your cousin?" I had to know I didn't make a mistake by going there.

"Like I told you before, fuck her. Just because we have the same blood doesn't mean that I'm loyal to that girl," he informed me. "Where ya man?"

I didn't know if he was trying to be funny or not. "Umm, I've been single for two months now, but I left him in the house with his bitch." I was starting to get angry all over again.

"So he was there when you shot her?" he asked sounding a little shocked.

"Yeah, he sent me a text telling me he had something important to tell me, so I walked in the house and guess who was there."

He just shook his head. "Wow, so do you need me to take you to your brother's house? I don't think you're in any condition to be driving."

"I'm not tryna be around him right now, we're just going to end up getting into it and I don't think that's healthy for the baby."

Kamil just looked at me sideways. It was then that I realized he was the only one besides Mykell that I hadn't told about the baby. *That's probably why Mone keeps blowing my phone up. Well that and the fact that I just shot somebody.*

Kamil interrupted my thoughts. "So you're pregnant again?"

"Unfortunately, yes."

"Are you keeping it?" He had a look of concern on his face.

"Yes, my baby didn't ask to be made, so it shouldn't have to pay for Mykell and mine's problems. Plus, in the spur of the moment, I kind of told him that my baby would be calling another nigga daddy. He should just look at it as one less child to worry about since Kya's pregnant."

His eyes damn near popped out his head when I said that. "She's what?"

"Pregnant." I laughed at the look on his face. "But enough about that. I need somewhere to lay my head and I was wondering if I could get my job back, Boss Man." I batted my eyes.

"You can stay here as long as you want, but I don't think a club is a good place for a pregnant woman to be working at, Fat Mama." He laughed and I punched him in the arm.

"I'm not even big yet and you're already calling me Fat Mama," I pouted playfully.

"Yo, but you greedy as hell."

"Whatever, but I want to apologize," I started and he cut me off.

"No, I owe you an apology. I didn't tell you that she was my cousin because I didn't want you to feel like you couldn't talk to me. I never meant to hurt you."

"It's cool Boss Man, and you can make it up to me by cooking dinner. Now get to it!" I hit him on the butt and laughed.

I would be lying if I said I hadn't missed Kamil the past two months. He was really fun to be around; he was silly and willing to do anything to make me smile or laugh.

Mykell

I couldn't believe Reneice's crazy ass pulled a gun out on me; I was even more shocked that she shot Kya. I knew I should be feeling bad but I wasn't. She had gotten what she deserved. Besides, as Neicey said, it was only a flesh wound. A little ointment and a couple of gauze pads and she would be straight. She shouldn't have been popping off at the mouth. Usually, I would intervene in situations like that; end that shit before it could even start. I didn't because I knew Neicey could handle her own and I wasn't expecting it to get to that level. Kya should have been a good side bitch and stayed in her place, but nope she had gotten her position mixed up. That shit was way out of line, what she had said about Neicey being raped.

I called Mone and Mack to come over because we had a lot of shit to discuss. That picture and phone call had fucked me all the way up. It had been two months since some grimy niggas took my son. I had a feeling they were the same niggas that had something to do with Neicey being raped. I could feel it in my gut. About twenty minutes later, those happy go lucky niggas came walking through the door. The look my brother gave me told me he knew something wasn't right with me. "Talk to me Kell."

I just shook my head and looked at Mone. "What did she do now?" he asked already knowing it was about his sister.

"Her ass done came up in here and shot Kya."

"Why the fuck would you have Kya over here when you knew you told Neicey to come over here?" Mack asked scolding me.

"Man, yo check this out. I did not, I repeat, I did not invite that bitch over here. The doorbell rang so I was thinking it was Neicey tryna be funny by not using her key. I opened the door and that bitch was standing there smiling like the damn Joker. I told her ass to leave and she got to popping off at the mouth. Neicey showed up and walked in, but she was calm about everything. Until Kya said, it was her own fault she was raped. That's when all hell broke loose. Neicey was looking fucking possessed yo!"

"She didn't! So what baby girl do?" Mack asked like I was telling the best story ever.

"Nigga, I told you she shot her. Straight whipped the gun out so fast I didn't see where she got it. She started praying then POP! Thank God it was only a flesh wound." I looked over at Mone and he didn't even seem fazed about what I was saying.

"Damn Money Mone yo sister a real thoroughbred! I didn't know she got down like that," Mack said.

"One of my homeboys used to take her to the shooting range when he was supposed to be watching her after school. By the time I found out, it was too late. I knew she had a badass temper on her, so I never put a gun in her hands. When I asked him why he did it, he told me, and I fully understood." He shrugged as if it was nothing.

"Nigga, would you like to let us in on why he did it?" I asked trying to figure that shit out.

"If I tell you, she'll kill me."

"C'mon now man, we don't run our mouths like bitches."

"Aight," he said and took a deep breath. "He did it because this nigga that lived in our neighborhood was a pervert. Neicey got tired of me and my niggas following her everywhere, so one day she didn't tell us that she had a half-day at school. While she was walking home, he tried to grab her and rape her, but he didn't know who he was fucking with. She fought him like I taught her to and she got away. She went home, found one of my guns, and went looking for the nigga. She found him and put a bullet right in the middle of his forehead. My Ladybug caught her first body at the age of nine. She told my boy and he started taking her to the shooting range. After that, she ain't never been the same. Then two years later, we lost our mom, and that didn't help none."

Damn, I didn't know she had issues like that. I had thought she was just hot headed but she was actually hurting. *I feel like shit because I didn't do anything but add to the pain.* Damn man.

"Mone, let me see yo phone real fast," I said. I knew if I called from my phone, she wouldn't answer. I called her and it rung two times before going straight to voicemail.

"Damn man," I said giving Ramone his phone back. I just knew she would answer if she saw his name pop up on her phone. I just had to talk to her and let her know that shit wasn't what it seemed. We had worked through everything else, so I knew that wouldn't be any different. I would just give her some time to cool off.

Kamil

It had been four weeks since Reneice walked through my door and she had been by my side ever since. I loved having her around and I hoped she never left. We were lying around watching TV when her phone rang. She looked at the phone funny and then answered. "Uh, hello?"

I was listening intently to the one-sided conversation. "Right now? Are you sure?" She jumped off the couch. "Alright thank you so much, I'm on the way."

I got up right along with her. I was confused as to what was going on but I was ready for whatever. "What's up?"

"We need to get to the hospital, NOW!" She ran for the door.

On the way to the hospital, she kept mumbling about some nigga not ever answering his phone when it was important. I figured she was talking about that bitch nigga Mykell. Sometimes I wondered if she really knew who I was or what I was about, would she still fuck with me? *Why the fuck not, I'm no different than her ex nigga.*

I knew it would only be a matter of time before that nigga would fuck up, which meant that I would luck up. She told me we were going to have to take it slow, which was fine with me. I didn't even give a fuck about her being pregnant with that nigga's baby. I didn't have a problem playing daddy. Especially to that nigga's baby since he already didn't care for a nigga.

We pulled up to the hospital and I followed her to a room. I saw a little boy lying in the bed, who I assumed was that nigga's son. No lie, lil man looked just like his daddy. I stayed back by the door while Neicey talked to the doctor. The doctor gave the okay on everything, gave her his discharge papers, and we were out of there.

We all got in the car and I asked lil man if he was hungry. He said yeah, so I headed out to get something to eat. He waited a few minutes before he asked the million-dollar question. "Are you my mommy's boyfriend?"

I didn't know how to answer that question so I looked at Neicey for help. "Maybe, if he plays his cards right, and if my lil man approves."

"Hi, I'm MJ, the man of her life." I laughed because I used to be the same way about my mom, overprotective.

"Wassup, lil man, I'm Kamil."

"MJ, you know me and your dad are going to sit down and have a talk with you about what happened. But I'ma let you rest today."

"Alright Mommy."

We went out to eat and the more I hung around little man, the more I liked him. It would be real petty of me to have a problem with him or not like him just because his dad and I had a problem with each other. I sat back and watched in amazement at how Neicey interacted with lil man. She had stepped in at eighteen years old and played the mother role to him. I knew it had to be hard sometimes seeing how she lost her mom, but she did an excellent job.

Someday I wanted that for us. To see her be a mother to my kids. I knew I said I would play daddy to that nigga's baby, but I didn't think a man should ever miss out on raising their kids. Shit, my donor was never there for me. My mama taught my brothers and me how to be men, something she should have never had to do. I was going to have to talk to her about that situation.

Kya

That bitch done fucked with the wrong one. I couldn't believe she shot my ass, but where she messed up at was not killing me. The other day, some chick approached me with an offer to helping me take that bitch Reneice down. She would rather do business over the phone because she didn't want to meet up face to face anymore. I said fuck it, why not? My other resource had been slipping. In due time, I would expose their ass for the snake they really were.

Reneice

Before we left the restaurant, Kamil pulled me to the side to talk to me. "You know I did some thinking, and you should allow Mykell to be in his baby's life. I know you're mad at him, but like you said, your baby shouldn't have to suffer because you two don't want to be together. If you intentionally keep your child from him, he or she might grew up and resent you."

Ugh! Curse that man for being so damn fine and smart. He was right though, even if I did hate to admit it. I didn't want my child being mad at me. I knew what it was like not to have a father so why would I put my child through the same thing? Damn, damn, damn. See that was why I kept him around, he helped me make decisions.

I sighed heavily. "Alright Mil Mil. I hear you; I'll take that into consideration."

"That's all I ask that you do." He kissed my forehead and flashed that sexy smile that I was starting to fall in love with. My mind flashed back to MJ's question. *Do I consider Kamil as my boyfriend? Would it be too soon to be in another relationship, especially while I'm pregnant? Would my child be confused about who its father was?* So many thoughts were clouding my mind.

After we took MJ out to eat, it was time to take him to his father. It had been a month since I'd been in that house. I really didn't want to be there but it was not about me. It was about MJ. I unlocked the door with my key and didn't miss the displeased look that I got from Kamil. Whatever, as long as I had a child, well, two children by that nigga, I would use that key whenever I wanted until he asked for it back.

I walked expecting to see something I didn't want to see and I didn't. Well, I kind of did. Mykell was knocked out on the couch in the den in some basketball shorts and no shirt. His ass looked so sexy; I almost forgot what I was here for. I hit him on the chest and the nigga jumped up with wild eyes.

"Surprise!" I laughed.

"You finally decided to come home?"

"Nope, but I have something for you."

Kamil walked in the room holding a sleeping MJ. He fell asleep on the ride there. Mykell didn't look too happy to see Kamil holding his son but what... the... fuck... ever! "His room is up the stairs to,"

Mykell cut me off. "Nah, I've got him. I don't know this nigga like that to be letting him all up in my house."

I just rolled my eyes at that nigga. He was just jealous. *He fucked up, so I'ma let a real nigga make it right.* He came back down the stairs and mugged Kamil, then turned his attention to me. "Wassup, *baby mama*, how you been doing?" he asked smartly. I just knew he didn't have an attitude.

"I'm fine baby daddy how are you?" I decided to play nice.

"Wonderful now that I have my son back. Where did you find him?"

"Actually, he found me. The hospital called and told me he's been there for three days. They tried calling you and couldn't get an answer, so MJ gave them my number."

"Thank you."

"You don't have to thank me for taking care of my son."

There was an awkward silence in the air. I looked over at Kamil who was standing by the door acting incognito. He gave me a reassuring head nod. I took a deep breath and said what I had to say.

"I have a doctor's appointment once a month because of the pregnancy. My next one is in two weeks and I thought you should be there seeing as how you are the father." It felt like it took all my breath away to tell him that. I didn't know why I was looking at the ground all nervous and shit. I had been in love with that man, he was my first, and even though I was not in love with him anymore, I still loved him. It was kind of crazy.

He walked up to me and lifted my head, "Why you looking at the ground? So does this mean when I call you're gonna answer? I understand you don't want to be with me, I got that part, but I at least want to be in my child's life. And I still want you to be in MJ's life. I know you moved on and I can accept that. Let's just be parents to our children and put all the bullshit behind us."

He stuck out his hand for me to shake so we could call a truce. I just laughed and we shook on it.

"I told MJ that we need to sit down and have a talk with him about the incident, but I didn't want to do it today. I just wanted him to enjoy being back home. So call me when y'all are ready to have that talk."

"Aight."

I left Mykell's house feeling better than I did when I got there. I didn't know what to expect when I went in there. I was happy that we were on good terms for the sake of our children, that's what was important.

I noticed Kamil was quiet and that was unusual for him. I had to know what was up with him. "Wassup? Talk to me."

"Help me figure something out real quick."

"What?"

"Why do you still have keys to that nigga's shit?"

I was a little taken aback by his question and the way he asked it. *I just know his ass is not jealous.* "Because he hasn't asked for it back yet," I said thinking it was no big deal.

"Is that right?"

"Sure is!"

"He shouldn't have to. The moment you left that nigga, you should have given him his keys back."

"Why? What's the big deal about me having keys to his house? I've had the key for almost three years. Hell, I had a key before I even moved in. If he didn't want me to have a key to his house anymore, I know for a fact that he wouldn't hesitate to ask for it back." I was getting annoyed with the conversation. He was tryna make a big deal out of nothing.

Mykell

I met a girl about a month earlier named Lisa. She was not Neicey and she damn sure didn't have shit on her, but she helped me keep my mind off her. Pops called and told me he was having a little get together at his house since it had been awhile since we'd all gotten together. I asked him if it was cool if I invited shorty and he said yeah.

"So I'm meeting the family already huh?" she asked on the way to the house. I looked at her before answering, "Uh yeah I guess so."

I hope her ass don't get the wrong impression. I'm not even tryna go there with her ass. Hell she gotta get through Lani's crazy ass before she even thinks she's in the family.

When I got to the house Mack, Lani, Mone, and Pops were chilling. When I saw Ramone, I remembered that Neicey might be coming. *Damn, I forgot all about her, I wonder how this shit gonna play out.*

I saw Lani looking at Lisa funny and knew she was gonna be on some other shit. She just didn't want to like her because she wasn't Neicey. "Wassup everybody, this is Lisa. Lisa, that's my dad, my baby sister Lani and my two brothers Micah and Ramone."

It was dead ass quiet for a minute; everybody was looking at me as if I was crazy. Finally Pops spoke up, "Hi Lisa, nice to meet you."

"Nice to meet you too, all of you."

"My other sister should be here soon, and then it should get real interesting in here. We're the queens of this family," Lani said. I couldn't even be mad at her because she had always been that way whenever Mack and I had females around.

We were in the basement in the theater room for about twenty minutes before I heard the front door close. "Pop-Pop!" *Oh shit, here we go.*

"Aw shit, my sisters here!" Lani gave me a dirty look, and I gave her lil ass one right back.

Neicey waddled her pregnant ass down the stairs with MJ. She was now five months pregnant and at her last appointment we found out she was having a boy. To say I was happy would be an understatement. I couldn't help but smile at her. She was glowing and her hair was growing like mad.

"Okay everybody, the life of the party is here so let's get it cracking."

"It's about time yo fat butt got here, we've been waiting on you forever."

"Mack don't even go there! If yo nephew wasn't sitting on my bladder I would have made it on time," she said and laughed.

"MJ, you not gonna speak? You've been around Neicey all day and now you acting funny. She's starting to rub off on you," I joked.

"Hi Dad." He kept it short and I just shook my head.

"Don't even go there punk." Neicey threw a pen at me.

"You have a son?" Lisa asked. Neicey looked at her like she just noticed her for the first time.

"Oh, let me do the introductions," Lani said. "Lisa, this is Neicey my sister, Neicey this is Lisa she's Mykell's. . ."

"Girlfriend," Lisa cut Lani off. I looked at her like she was crazy and Lani looked at her like she was ready to beat her ass. "Hi, are you the baby sister?" she asked her.

"Something like that, I'm the baby and he," Neicey said pointing at me, "he's the father of my child."

Before I could say anything, that bitch ass nigga came down the stairs. "Wassup everybody."

"Hey Kamil," everybody spoke but me.

He hit Neicey on the ass, "I thought I told you to wait for me Fat Mama."

"I know but you were taking too long." She giggled like a damn schoolgirl.

"I need a fucking drink," Ramone said getting off the couch and heading upstairs. That was my cue. "Make that two," I said following him.

"How about three," Mack followed suit. I knew Pops wasn't going to leave Lani down there with Lisa and I knew that nigga wasn't about to leave Neicey's side.

When we got upstairs to the kitchen, Ramone went in.

"She just gonna bring that nigga up in here like he family or something. Then she looked right at me and didn't even speak. Her ass been acting real funny towards me for a couple of months and I'm tired of the shit," he said, pouring himself a glass full of Hennessey.

"You know what I think?" Mack asked not giving us time to answer. "I think y'all on some other shit. You knew she was going to be here and she knew you were going to be here, but y'all both brung y'all rebounds just to get a rise out of each other. Well it looks like Neicey won because she don't give a fuck about ol girl down there but the moment you saw my mans, yo ass got the fuck on."

"What the fuck ever *Micah,* ain't nobody thinking bout that nigga. I just don't like him being around my son, hell both of my sons."

"Well, if you would've been taking care of home, he wouldn't have to be around. Period." That nigga was starting to act like Pops.

"Mack, I hear what you're saying and all, that's my baby sister; hell my only sister, but I don't agree with this bullshit she has going on. As soon as she left Mykell, she moved in with the nigga, the exact same day. So something is telling me that she was already fucking the nigga. So Kell, if I was you I would get a blood test on that baby."

I had to look at that nigga to make sure I was hearing him right. Was he saying that his sister wasn't carrying my baby? I just knew that nigga was already drunk. I could smell the liquor on his breath the moment I walked through the door. No matter what he said, I knew for a fact, that Reneice was having *my* son.

Reneice

I sat there with Mykell's new girlfriend to feel her out. I had to know who was going to be around MJ.

"So, you're Mykell's son?" she asked MJ

MJ looked at her up and down, "Who are you?"

"Your daddy's girlfriend."

"My daddy don't got no girlfriend. He loves my mommy."

"MJ, that's enough."

"But Mommy…"

"No buts, go pick a movie for us to watch."

I looked over a Lisa and she was already looking at me.

"So how long have you and Mykell been together?"

"A month."

Lani chuckled at her statement. "What makes you think you're his girlfriend? Because we have never heard nothing about you and any chick that tries to get in this family needs my approval."

"Le'Lani," Pop-Pop said. We all turned to look at him. For a minute, I'd forgotten he was down there. He was so quiet.

"I'm just saying Daddy. He didn't introduce her to us as his girlfriend earlier."

"Leave it alone." That was exactly what she did; nobody went against what Pop-Pop said.

"So, is that his baby too?" she asked pointing at my stomach.

"Yes that's my little brother," MJ said coming to hand me a movie. "Here Mommy, put this one in. We used to watch this all the time."

"Boyz in the Hood," I laughed. "Of course sweetie."

"I got it baby," Kamil said getting up to put the movie in.

"Kamil, can I sit on your lap since, I can't sit on Mommy's because of Daddy."

I laughed. "Oh my God, this boy is seven going on 37."

MJ climbed on Kamil's lap and Pop-Pop dimmed the lights. I could feel Lisa's eyes burning a hole in the side of my face. I looked over at Lani and she gave me a knowing look. It was funny how we could communicate with each other without words.

Ten minutes later, the three stooges decided to come downstairs. Everybody took a seat except for Ramone. That nigga stood right in front of me wobbling. I knew he was drunk, he could never hold his liquor. "Mone, move out of the way. I'm tryna watch the movie."

He just stood there looking stupid. "Move, I'm not playing with you." He continued to stand there.

"Ramone, leave her alone and have a seat." Pop-Pop came to my defense.

"Pop I just wanna ask her a question," he slurred and wobbled a little. "Is that Mykell's baby or this nigga's baby?" He pointed from my stomach to Kamil.

"Ramone, you are out of bounds right now. Sit down somewhere with that bullshit," Lani intervened.

I laughed at that nigga. "Ramone Tyshaun Peake, if you don't get yo drunk ass out my face we gonna have a situation up in this bitch."

"Ramone, I said sit down," Pop-Pop's voiced roared through the room.

He walked away, or should I say, wobbled away, mumbling under his voice. "Nigga, if you have something to say, say that shit out loud. Don't talk under yo breath like a bitch," I snapped.

"It's always about yo little spoiled ass! You act like the world revolves around you. Yo lil ass is the reason my damn daddy left. Yo lil ungrateful ass is the reason I did a bid."

"Ramone, what the fuck are you talking about? You were locked up because you got caught with a gun, dumbass. And your daddy left because he was a bitch ass nigga. Right now you acting just like his ass," I yelled because that nigga was pissing me off. Kamil put his hand on my thigh to try to calm me down.

"Correction, Ladybug," he said walking back in front of me. "Daddy left because he didn't want any more kids and when he found out mama was pregnant with you it pissed him off! Oh, as far as the gun? That was the gun you shot that nigga with and the bitch was registered in my name. Yo stupid ass thought you were hiding it but you didn't do it right. I only did the little time I did because I had an alibi that didn't put me at the scene of the murder. I should have let the damn system take yo ass."

I jumped up in the nigga's face. "You right bitch, you should have let the system take my ass. Then I wouldn't have been raised by a bitch made nigga. After all the shit I did for yo ass, this how you do me? I've been damn near taking care of myself since mommy died. All that money you and yo boys used to give me, I never spent it. I kept it in a safe in my room and when I got old enough, I put it in a bank account. I was saving that for you, I never needed it. I was working at the little corner store with Mr. Jimmy and he would pay me under the table.

"Every time I got some money, I put it in that account. When I got a check from work or school, I put half in the bank. There's about $90,000 in that bank account right now. But yo ass don't deserve shit! I'll give that shit to MJ before I give yo dog ass shit!" I was hurt. I couldn't believe my only brother had that much malice in his heart for me. The fact that he said he should have let the system take me; that was just too much for me.

Before I knew it, he reached back and slapped the shit out my ass and I fell to the ground, that was how hard he hit me. I saw Micah, Mykell, and Pop-Pop get up and grab Ramone.

Click Clack. Lani was helping me off the floor when I looked up to see Kamil pointing his gun at Ramone. "Nigga if you ever in yo life put yo hands on my girl, I will kill you without a doubt. The only reason I'm not doing it now is because yo ignorant ass is drunk and I don't know how Neicey would feel about me laying yo ass out. But try some shit like that again and it lights out, for good."

"AHHHH!" I felt a sharp pain in my stomach. "Mommy what's wrong?"

"Kamil, put the gun down son, it's cool I've got it. You just get Neicey," Pop-Pop said while he still had Ramone hemmed up.

"Come on ma, get up." He reached down for my hand.

I grabbed his hand and tried to get up but the pain was too powerful.

"AHHH! I can't move Mil. UGHH!"

He bent down and scooped me up in his arms. "It's happening again. I'm gonna lose this baby too," I cried. "Why does this keep happening to me?"

"Shh don't say that ma," Kamil said. "You and little man are gonna be alright. I'm bout to take y'all to the hospital right now.

"We'll meet you there, after I handle this," said Pop-Pop.

I looked over at Mykell as Kamil carried me to the stairs. I saw something I'd never seen in his eyes before, fear. He was just as scared as I was. "AHHH!"

"I'm hurrying baby."

* * *

I was lying in the hospital bed thinking about what happened a few minutes earlier. I couldn't believe Ramone and I went at it like that. My lip was swollen and sore. We used to fight all the time, but he would just put me in a headlock until I said I was sorry. Then we would act as if nothing ever happened. However, that time was different. I was straight on him; I didn't care if he was my brother. Fuck him; I didn't need him around me if he felt that way. My thoughts were interrupted when everyone walked in the room. I was shocked to see Lisa walk through the door. I'd forgotten she was even there.

"Hey mami, how you doing?" Lani asked

"I'm good boo, they just said the baby was a little shaken up but he's okay."

Mykell came to my bed and rubbed my stomach. "Lil dude, don't scare Daddy like that. You had me worried for a minute there."

Then MJ came and did the same thing as his daddy. "Yeah baby brother, don't scare me like that, you almost made me put the paws on somebody. You're my baby brother so I have to look out for you and mommy, but Pop-Pop wouldn't let me get to him."

Everybody in the room laughed. That was exactly what I needed. I smiled when I saw all the people I loved the most by my side.

"The doctor said he wants to keep her here for a few days to keep an eye on her and the baby. He also wants to put her on bed rest until her next doctor's appointment," Kamil informed everybody. "He also said she needs to refrain from things that could be stressful and he wants her to take it easy."

My lip was hurting so bad. I put my hand up to it to feel how big it was. "You don't have to worry about that little incident that happened tonight. I took care of that and took his drunk ass home," Pop-Pop assured me.

"Thanks Pop-Pop," I said with tears falling from my eyes. MJ wiped my tears away, "Don't cry mommy. It's going to be okay."

I pulled my baby up in the bed with me and kissed his cheeks. It was crazy how much I loved that little boy. I loved him just like I'd birthed him. My baby must have felt his brother's presence because he started moving. I gasped because that as the first time I'd felt him move like that. I put MJ's hand on my belly, "Come here Mykell."

He came over to the bed and I put his hand by MJ's. They baby moved again. MJ and Mykell both jumped. I just laughed. "That was your little brother," I pointed at MJ "and your son in there getting excited," I said pointing at Mykell.

"Whoa!" MJ leaned down to kiss my stomach.

I heard somebody clear their throat and everybody looked at Lisa.

"Ain't it time for you to go?" Lani asked with an attitude.

"When Mykell's ready, I'll leave."

"Well I'ma be here for a while, so get comfortable."

"Her boyfriend is over there. He can take care of her."

I looked over at Mykell and then back at Lisa. I saw his vein popping out his neck, so I knew he was mad.

"I'll take her home. I have some business to handle anyways. Baby girl, I'll see you tomorrow. Come on, MJ, you're hanging with me tonight," Pop-Pop said.

MJ gave me kiss before climbing out of the bed. "Bye Mommy, bye Dad. Love y'all"

'Bye," we said in unison.

I looked back at Lisa, she gave me the evil eye before walking out the door, and I smirked. Mykell didn't even look her way.

Chapter 2

Ramone

I woke up that next morning feeling like shit. I looked over and I didn't see my shorty, so I went downstairs to look for her. I saw her sitting at the dining room table with a plate of food in front of her. "Where's mine?" She just looked at me and rolled her eyes. I knew she was probably pissed at me. I was mad at myself, shit got too out of hand because of me. "I've got a real bad hangover and I need you to take care of me."

"I'm not doing shit for you," she said with an attitude.

"C'mon Le'Lani, I know I fucked up! Pops already damn near cracked my jaw," I said putting my hand to my sore jaw.

"You better be glad that's all he did. You embarrassed your only sister in front of everybody. You basically said that wasn't Mykell's baby she was carrying, slapped her for no reason, and then put her in the hospital."

My heart dropped when she said that. I didn't know she was in the hospital. "She's in the hospital? W-w-what's wrong? She okay? Is the baby okay?" I got out in one breath.

"How nice of you to care," she said sarcastically. "She's fine, the doctors want to keep her for a few days to monitor the baby, then when she's released they want to basically put her on bed rest until her next doctor's appointment next month."

"Well that's good."

"Yup. I'm going up there to see her later and you're coming with me. Then you can finally tell her about us after you apologize, since you messed that up last night too."

"I don't think she wants to see me Lani," I sighed rubbing my head.

"Well that's just too damn bad! You're going to see your sister whether either one of you likes it or not."

I just sat there and thought back to when Lani and I first got together.

I was chilling at Mykell's house waiting for him to get back to the house when Lani walked in the house looking sexy as hell.

"Hey Mone, what's up?" she asked.

"You," I replied.

She just laughed. "You so silly," she said coming to sit by me on the couch.

"I'm serious. So wassup? You got a man or something?"

"Why?" she asked.

"I already told you I'm trying to get with you."

"The last time I checked you had a girl and a baby on the way," she said, eyeing me.

"The baby I don't know about, but shit, I'm single."

She just shook her head. "Since when?"

"Today," I said with a smirk.

"So how you trying to get with me after only being single for one day?"

"Because I see something I like and want, and a nigga like me always gets what he wants."

"Is that right?"

"I wouldn't lie to you."

She looked at me as if she didn't believe me. "Look Le'Lani, I raised my sister and I know how I would feel and what I would do if somebody hurt her so I'm not in the business of hurting women. All I'm asking is for a chance ma, you can do that can't you?"

Now there we were. I loved her lil bossy smart mouth ass.

*   *   *

When we got to the hospital, I got nervous. I felt really bad about what happened. When we walked in, I was surprised to see Mykell there and not ol boy. "Hey mami," Lani said walking further in the room.

"Hey boo," Neicey smiled. Her smile faded when she saw me. *I knew I shouldn't have come.*

"So. . ." Lani started but Ladybug cut her off staring at me.

"Hold up Lani. How you gonna just walk in my room and not speak to me? Even though I really don't fuck with you right now and I just ought to beat yo ass, all bullshit aside, you're still my brother."

"Hey Ladybug," I said nervously.

"Mhm,"

"Wassup Kell?"

"Nothing much man, just up here with my son and his mother." He looked like he wanted to say more but his cell phone rang. He looked at it and put it back in his pocket.

"Mykell stop sending that girl to voicemail. This is the fourth time she's called you since you've been here and it's only been an hour. Just call the girl," Niecey fussed.

"I'm straight." he replied.

"Ugh where did you pick up that rat anyways? And who told her to introduce herself as your *girlfriend*? I almost slapped the taste out her mouth," Lani fumed

"I don't know where she got that from, but I picked her up from the liquor store because this one right here wanna be on games."

Ladybug rolled her eyes. "Anyways when were y'all going to tell me y'all got together? I mean I should have been the first person to know."

"How did you know?" I asked shocked

"I'm your sister and her best friend, I know things."

"We were supposed to tell you last night, but you know how that went," Lani pushed me.

I cleared my throat. "Ladybug, I'm beyond sorry about last night. I don't know what came over me and I shouldn't have acted like that nor should I have put my hands on you. I know you're mad at me and I also know how long you take to forgive people but I truly am sorry and I love you."

"Apology accepted, but I'm still mad at you."

I just laughed because she could be so stubborn but I loved her.

Reneice

Being seven months pregnant sucked! I felt as big as a house. My feet were always swollen and I had some bad back pains, but in the end, it would all be worth it when I saw my lil man's face. Mykell sent me a text asking me to meet him at the Hilton downtown. I didn't think anything of it since we were both in committed relationships. I pulled up to the hotel, gave my name at the desk, and asked them to tell Mykell I was there. To my surprise, they gave me a room key, room number, and told me to go right up. *Okay that's a little weird.*

I headed up to the 10th floor, thank God for elevators. When I got to the room, I used my key to grant me access. When I went in, I saw a big plate of chocolate covered strawberries. I immediately headed that way. I was so busy stuffing my face that I didn't even notice Mykell come in the room.

"Lil greedy ass!" I jumped at the sound of his voice.

"Shut up! Wassup baby daddy?"

"Not shit just tryna spend some time with my favorite baby mama," he chuckled.

"If these strawberries weren't so good I'd throw one at yo head. Anyways where's wifey at?"

"I sent my *girlfriend* to go visit her parents for a week. Where's that nigga that wanna be me so bad?"

I just rolled my eyes at him. "Out," I kept it short and simple.

He pulled the chair from the desk and placed in towards the end of the bed. "Come here," he said while sitting in the chair.

I sat on the bed so he could pull my shoes off and rub my feet. "Why out of all the places to meet, did you pick a hotel?" I wanted to know, still stuffing my face with strawberries. He didn't answer my question but just sat there staring at me.

After of few more minutes of his staring game he decided to say something. "Are you really happy with that nigga?"

"Yes I am." My eyes never left his.

"Do you love him? And don't lie."

"Of course I do." Honestly, that was only partially the truth. Yes, I did love Kamil, but I wasn't in love with him. *Yet.*

I could have sworn I saw a flash of hurt in his eyes. "Do you love ol girl?"

He looked me in my eyes and said, "No, because I still love you, no scratch that, I'm still in love with you." After all those months of not being together, I still got hypnotized by his beautiful light brown eyes. So much that I didn't even feel him unbuckling my pants until he unzipped them. Then I finally came to my senses. I jumped back, got off the bed, and headed towards the door, not realizing I didn't have my shoes on. When I reached the door, he grabbed my arm and pushed my back against the door. Forcefully, but not too much that it would hurt the baby or me.

He looked in my eyes and again I was hypnotized. *Why the fuck does he always do that shit and why the fuck am I so weak?* Someway, somehow, he managed to get my pants off. He tried to kiss me, but I turned my head. He smirked at me mischievously, and I knew I was in for a world of trouble.

Mykell

I knew exactly what I was doing when I told Neicey to meet me there. Her bitch ass nigga was always around and Lisa's clingy ass was always up under me. That was why I sent her ass away for a week. Neicey was tryna act as if she didn't love me anymore, but I knew differently. I saw it in her eyes when she looked at me. She pissed me off when she said she loved that nigga, no lie that hurt a nigga's heart. But I was there to let her know I was not giving up that easily. Shit, I was supposed to be the *only* nigga she would ever love. I was the first to hit it and I knew damn well she better not be fucking that nigga while she was carrying my son.

I lifted her small ass up against the wall, even though she pregnant her ass was still light to me. Her legs wrapped around my head and I went in. I loved the fact that she didn't have any panties on, *makes my job a whole lot easier.*

I worked my tongue real fast on her clit, and then I sucked on it. I then stuck my tongue in her opening and fucked her with my tongue. She started shaking and I went faster. Then she did something she'd never done, she squirted; right in my mouth. I smirked because I knew my tongue game was the shit. Never mind the fact that she was only one woman I'd ever went down on and the only woman I would *ever* go down on.

I lowered her a little and unbuckled my pants; I was already hard as fuck so he just popped right out. I lowered her onto my throbbing dick and I felt her tense up. It had been almost a year since I'd been inside her. I kissed her neck and lightly bit it. I started pumping in and out of her and I felt her relax. She had tears in her eyes, I went in to kiss her and that time she didn't turn her head. I knew I had her then. Her belly was in the way so I couldn't fuck her how I really wanted.

I carried her over to the bed and bent her over standing up with her hands on the edge of the bed. "I hate you Mykell," she said, out of breath. I just smirked and slapped her on the ass. I pumped in and out of her as fast as I could without hurting her or my son. The nigga that said pregnant pussy is the best pussy ain't never lied. "Shut the fuck up! When you playing house with that nigga think about this," I said before I did one big thrust.

"Ahh....uh...stupid....mutha..." All I could do was laugh. She knew that nigga couldn't do her like I could. "If you make me go into labor... I'ma kill you! Uhn!" She was talking shit and moaning at the same time. I grabbed a handful of her hair; she turned and gave me the evil eye. I knew she hated that shit but that was just too damn bad. She was going to be punished; I found her G-Spot and pounded on it unmercifully. She screamed out while at the same time squirting. I felt her juices raining down.

"Uhh! My… Kell stooop," she hollered out. "Tell me that you still love me and I'll stop," I said still pounding. I was tired of playing those games with her; it was time for her to come home. I knew I messed up and I'd apologized a million times for it. What more did she want me to do?

"I don't hear you. Say it and I'll stop."

"I ugh... I love you!" That was all I needed to hear. That right there took me to my limit and it felt like my dick was leaking buckets. If she wasn't already pregnant, I might have just knocked her up with triplets.

I turned her around and she laid on her back trying to catch her breath. I just stood back looking at her. I was willing to do whatever it took to have my family back, even if that meant I had to off that bitch ass nigga. I sat on the bed beside her and placed my hand on her stomach. Instantly my lil man started moving and kicking. It was as if he knew his daddy was touching him. A big smile came across my lips but it was short-lived when I heard Neicey's sniffling. *Here we go.*

"What's wrong with you, man?" I asked knowing she was about to say some bullshit. She sat up and looked at me with tears in her eyes.

"Why did you bring me here Mykell? You think you accomplished something by fucking me? You claim you've changed but I can't tell. Now I've betrayed the one person who's had my back no matter what. Thanks a lot."

The shit that just came out her mouth had me boiling. "What the fuck you mean you don't think I've changed? You won't even give a nigga a chance to prove himself. And fuck that nigga! He wasn't the one there for you when you were depressed and wouldn't eat. He wasn't the one running and picking up yo medicine. He wasn't the one trying to do anything he could to bring you back to yo normal self." *Fuck she mean?*

"Actually he was there. He might not have been there physically because he didn't want to disrespect you, but he was there emotionally. He called every day to check on me, when I didn't answer, he would text me. Even though I wouldn't text back, every day he would text me something to let me know I was on his mind. As far as you being a changed man, I know for a fact that that's not true because you doing the same thing to Lisa that you did to me! You in a 'relationship' with her, but you tricked your ex into coming to a hotel room so you could have sex with her. So please tell me how you've changed?"

Damn, no lie, that shit she said about Lisa was true; I understood what she meant, but fuck that. The fact that she would throw what that nigga did for her in my face was just foul. "I tricked you huh? Come on now Reneice; don't even pull that shit with me. You knew what the fuck was about to go down when I told you to meet me here. Tell the truth, you wanted it just as bad as I did. You still love me just as much as I love you."

She just dropped her head and looked at the floor. *Bingo, I got her ass.*

"Mykell, I can't go there with you. We're both in relationships. Yes, I love you and I always will, but I'm not in love with you anymore."

Damn, that was how she felt. *Have I lost her for good?* "So you're telling me you don't want me anymore?"

She just looked at the floor not answering my question. "Reneice," I used her real name to let her know I was serious. "Answer the damn question!"

"I-I can't."

"Why the hell not?"

"I just can't Mykell, damn!" By that point, she had tears running down her face. I just took her in my arms and held her. After a few minutes, I kissed her forehead, "Go hop in the shower real quick before ol boy get suspicious. I got you some clothes in that bag over there." I was feeling defeated. I didn't know what else to do to show her how much I loved her and really wanted to be with her. *Maybe we're really over.*

* * *

It had been three weeks since the incident at the hotel and Neicey had been avoiding a nigga like the plague. She wouldn't answer my calls or text and nobody had seen her. Lisa had been stressing a nigga out. Her ass really thought she was my girl, but I said otherwise. My lil man didn't even like her and if MJ said you're a no go, then your ass is a no go. On top of that, Kya's ass was in her last month of her pregnancy, so she was due any day. She'd been blowing a nigga's phone up all day, every day. As soon as she popped that baby out, I wanted a DNA test; hands down. That shit was necessary.

Kya

I was due any day and Mykell's ass was still playing around. I heard his bitch, or should I say ex-bitch, moved in with my cousin. How cute was that? I also heard Mykell got a new bitch. He just didn't get it. He belonged to me and me only! I thought because he and the broad weren't together anymore that my little friend would take the hit off her head, but nope.

I was sitting there looking at the text she had just sent me.

Unknown: After that bitch drops that load, it's lights out for her ass. I might not even let the lil bastard live.

Now that was some harsh shit, to kill a baby. Really? I wanted the bitch dead myself because she shot me. I didn't give a damn if it was a flesh wound. But I didn't know if I could harm a baby. Especially since I was about to be a mother myself.

Reneice

Ever since that day at the hotel, I'd been trying my best to ignore Mykell. His ass always had to be the one to stir some shit up. Why couldn't he just be happy in his relationship and let me be happy in mine? Nope, he always had to have things his way, but not anymore.

It had been a couple of months since MJ had been home and we hadn't had that talk yet, so it was time to do it. I was two minutes away from Mykell's house when I called him.

"Hello?"

"I'm at the door."

"Use yo key," he said, a little too excited for me.

Yes, I still had the key to his house. He hadn't asked for it back so he must not have want it. It wasn't like I popped up at his house whenever I wanted to.

I walked in and MJ was in his favorite spot, in front of the TV with his game controller in his hand. "Don't you have some homework to do?" I joked.

"Hey Mommy!" He never took his eyes off the TV. I just shook my head. I went to the kitchen to see what there was to eat. It seemed like since I'd been pregnant I'd been eating everything and all the time. My son was going to be a greedy one, sad to say.

I was bent over looking in the refrigerator when I heard Mykell come in the kitchen. He whistled, "Nice view," he laughed.

"Oh yeah? Since you're back there how bout you kiss it," I said grabbing a Sprite and a yogurt.

"It'll be my pleasure too, but kissing it won't be the only thing I do to it," he smirked devilishly.

"Pervert," I said while opening the Sprite.

"But you like it," he said, taking the Sprite out my hands and drinking it. "My son doesn't need all this acid."

I rolled my eyes. "But I'm thirsty," I whined.

"There's some juice in there," he yelled leaving the kitchen. I followed behind him into the living room. I turned the TV off in the middle of MJ's game so I could get his attention.

"Aw c'mon, Mom! That's not fair!"

"Let's talk." I ignored him.

"About what?"

"What happened and what you remember about when you were taken from us."

"All I remember is I heard girly voices. I stayed in a little room the whole time and it had a big lock on it so I couldn't get out. It had a bed and bathroom in there and they would bring me food and stuff when I was asleep. I heard them talking about Daddy saying he was gonna pay."

"You said you heard girly voices?"

"Yes, they were girls."

I looked over and Mykell and he had a confused look on his face. *One of his bitches got mad at him and took my son.*

"How did you get away?" I asked.

"I was in the room playing. I jumped off the bed and hit the floor. When I woke up I was in the hospital and that's when you and Kamil came and got me."

"Okay baby, that's good enough. Turn the TV on and finish your game."

"Let me holla at you in the kitchen," Mykell said.

"Now you know you gotta help me off the couch." He laughed at me and helped me up.

We went to the kitchen and he spoke first. "I don't know who could have did that, you were the first female I messed with when I got out so this shit has me stuck."

"Maybe it's an ex-lover or something," I shrugged.

"Nah, I doubt that."

There was a knock at the door. "I'll get it, unless you mind," I said

"Man go on with that shit and get the door." He waved me off.

I waddled my pregnant ass to the door and opened it. *Here we go.* I said letting Lisa in. She looked at me up and down, like she had a problem. "Where's Mykell?" she asked with an attitude.

"Handling business, why are you here?" MJ asked before I could respond. That little boy was a hot ass mess. He'd been hanging around me too much.

She sucked her teeth. "Mykell! Something's at the door to see you." I smirked.

"Did you just call me a something?"

"Obviously you heard me."

"What are you doing here?" Mykell came saving that bitch from a beat down.

I walked over to the couch and sat down staring at the two.

"You didn't answer my calls, so I decided to see what was up, and now I know." She looked over at me.

"You got something you need to get off yo chest?" I was getting tired of that bitch and her attitude.

"Not at all, you just stay over there like a good baby mama."

"And you stay over there and try not to get yo ass whooped like a sorry ass jump off," I retorted.

"Alright, enough of that bullshit. Neicey you stay over there. You not beating nobody's ass while you're pregnant with my son."

"Oh," I snapped my fingers. "I forgot to tell you I picked out a name. His name is going to be Romell Zyin Jones."

"Where you pick that middle name from?" he asked with a big smile on his face.

"Big head right here," I said mushing MJ's head.

He laughed.

"I like that."

"Excuse me, but I am still standing here. Could you give us a moment of privacy please? Don't you have a man to go home to?"

"Yeah, but I'm here chilling with yours. And if you want to talk, you can take yo ass outside, that's where the trash belongs anyways."

"Good one Mommy," MJ laughed.

"Hush up Mykell Jr. and play yo game."

"I don't want to catch a case for hitting a pregnant woman."

"I'm not gonna be pregnant forever bitch. Holla at me in two more months."

"Cut that shit out! Now what do you want Lisa?" Mykell yelled.

"I just wanted to know why you were ignoring me."

"I'm not ignoring you, Lisa. I've just been busy handling family business."

"Oh yeah," she gave me another dirty look. *Let me get outta here before I fuck this bitch up.* "MJ come help your mom off the couch."

"Okay! Dad can I stay with Mom and Kamil tonight?"

"You know you have school tomorrow, and you ain't even looked at your homework since you got home," Mykell said busting him out.

"Mykell Jr. you better get yo lil butt up them stairs and do that homework before I act a fool," I fussed.

"Snitch," he looked at his dad then ran up the stairs laughing.

"Alright Mykell number one, I'm outta here. Call me and let me know if number two did his homework."

"Aight, I'll call you."

"You do that."

Kamil

I was really trying to be nice about that little situation with Reneice and that nigga. I understood that was the father of her child and everything but I didn't trust him. I knew she didn't have feelings for him anymore, but something told me he didn't feel the same way. I could tell that by the way he looked at her. He did little stuff to let me know he wasn't going anywhere. That was some bitch shit. But it wouldn't be long before she was popping out my baby.

I had been so wrapped up in her ass that I had been neglecting my work. If Neicey really knew what I did she probably wouldn't agree, but I knew she wouldn't judge me either. It just wasn't time for me to tell her yet.

I was sitting there waiting for her to bring her lil pregnant ass home. She told me she had to talk with MJ and Mykell about his disappearance. I respected that fact that she let a nigga know when she going to see him and wasn't sneaky about it.

I was lying in the bed watching TV when I heard the front door close. *My lil shorty is home.* I smiled thinking to myself how being patient really paid off. I finally got my girl and she wasn't going anywhere. "What you smiling about?" she asked walking over to me giving me a kiss on the lips.

"You," I smacked her ass.

"Oh yeah? What about me?"

"You just want me to gas yo head up, nosey," I chuckled.

"Duh," she said getting undressed and throwing on one of my t-shirts.

She laid on the bed and started rubbing her round belly. "Two more months lil man and Mommy can finally meet you! I hope you hurry up because all this heartburn you've been giving me ain't gonna cut it, Romell."

That was the first time I'd heard her say his name, I kinda liked it, I guess.

"Romell huh?"

"Yup, Romell Zyin. MJ helped me pick it out."

I was about to say something but her phone rang. "I'll get it," I said knowing she wasn't tryna get out of the bed. "Thanks babe," she replied with a smile.

"Hello."

"Where Neicey?"

I was thrown off by the male voice because I didn't look at the name before I answered.

"Who this?"

"Can I just talk to Reneice, damn."

I laughed knowing exactly who it was. "Baby, yo past is on the phone." I handed her the phone.

"Talk to me," she said into the phone.

"Uhn hunh."

"Yeah, alright. Give him a kiss and tell him I love him and I'll do the same to Romell."

"Kay, bye."

I took the phone and put it on the charger. "I'ma end up fucking yo baby daddy up!" I plopped down on the bed.

"Oh hush, he was just calling to let me know MJ finished his homework."

"Mhm."

"Romell, your daddy says he loves you and if I could kiss my belly I would." She laughed.

"Romell Zyin, I like that. Who's last name he taking?"

"Mykell's," she sighed.

"Oh, I guess."

I'll be happy when she has this baby so I can get some pussy.

Mykell

I got a call around 7:00 in the morning from Kya, saying her water broke and she wanted me to come to the hospital. I wasn't going to go, but what if that was my child and I wasn't there for the birth. By time I got to the hospital, she had already had the baby. *Damn,* she had a beautiful baby girl and she named her Destiny. She had a head full of hair. I pulled one of the nurses to the side and told them that I wanted a DNA test done. They took me to a room and swabbed my mouth. Then I went back to the room with Kya. I held Destiny in my arms but

I didn't feel that connection. She didn't look anything like me. I didn't even see any of my features on her.

I left out of the hospital not really wanting to be around Kya. She was asleep the whole time, which was great for me. I went to do what needed to be done.

I decided to pick MJ up from school early. He and I hadn't really been spending time together so I wanted to kick it with my lil man before his brother got there. "Hey Dad."

"Wassup, big head. You wanna kick it with me today?"

"Yeah, but don't tell Mommy, you know we would be in trouble," he said seriously.

I laughed at him. "Little man don't worry, I can handle your mom."

He got quiet for a minute and I knew something was up.

"What's on yo mind?"

"I don't like you and Mommy not being together. I like Kamil and all, but sometimes he does weird stuff. Besides I don't like Lisa, she's not mommy material and she's jealous of Mommy."

My son was too smart for his age. "What do you mean Kamil does weird stuff?"

"When I go over sometimes, he leaves in the middle of the night and you know Mommy sleeps like a bear. Or sometimes in the middle of the night, he would walk around whispering on the phone."

What the fuck, I need to put Neicey up on game. Nahh she probably won't believe me. I thought as I drove. I knew I didn't like that nigga. I needed to get some info on that nigga.

"You ready to meet yo lil brother?"

"Yes, I hope he looks like me."

"You mean like me?"

"No Dad, I look better so I hope me looks like *me.*"

I laughed at my little man, "Hate to break that lil heart of yours, but you look just like me."

"Don't insult me Dad."

"What?" I mushed his head and he gigged. I loved that lil boy with all my heart.

* * *

After spending time with my son, I decided to call Neicey.

"Talk to me!"

"I need to pick yo brain about something."

"Cool and I need to pick yo pockets. I was just about to go do some more baby shopping, wanna come?"

"Yeah, I need to see what you tryna make my son wear and see if I approve."

"Boy whatever, I've got good taste."

"I know because you picked me," I boasted.

She laughed like I told a joke or something. "Whatever, I'm on my way so you and yo lil mini-me be ready."

"Aight," I shook my head at that girl. "Yo MJ!"

"Yes."

"Ya mom on her way so we can do some shopping for the baby."

"Yayyy!"

Twenty minutes later Neicey pulled up. "Hey handsome."

"Hey sexy."

"I was talking to MJ, but hey to you too."

"Oh, okay, remember that."

"Just playing."

"Mommy, I saw some really cute baby boat shoes I want to get baby Mell," MJ interrupted.

"Alright, baby boy, let's shop till we drop!"

"Oh boy, what did I get myself into?" I asked with a laugh.

"You know I'm exactly eight months today. One more month and prince number two will be here."

"I wanna be there when you have him," MJ said excitedly.

"Of course, baby."

We pulled up at the Fairlane Mall and Neicey was too ready to do some shopping.

"Ohh look, it has a hat to go with it," she said holding up an outfit.

"Aw hell naw! My son will not be wearing that."

"Why not? It's cute." She pouted.

"Uhh no, put that back where you found it."

She rolled her eyes. "Fine."

We shopped for three hours. We finally took a break to get something to eat. "So when are you going to give me my black card back?" I asked knowing damn well I didn't care that she still had it.

"When you ask for it back."

"Yeah right."

"Naw, but fo real, I wanted to talk to you about some information that MJ shared with me. I'm not coming to you on no hating bullshit either."

"Okay, speak yo mind."

MJ and I shared our concerns with her and she just sat there looking stone-faced.

"Mommy are you mad at me?"

"No baby, you did exactly what you were supposed to do. Thank you," she kissed him on the cheek.

She then leaned over and did the same to me. I smiled on the inside; it had been awhile since I felt her lips. "Mommy when are you and Daddy getting back together?" MJ asked.

She shifted in her seat as if she was uncomfortable. "Umm I don't know baby. Mommy and Daddy have some serious issues that we need to work out before we can even think about getting back together."

I felt happy on the inside because she didn't say that we were never going to get back together. That right there just let me know that she still had feelings for me.

Chapter 3

Reneice

I was sleeping well. Until I was woken up out of my sleep by pain. I tried to move but the pain was too unbearable. I felt something wet between my legs, *no it can't be.* I looked to the other side of the bed and noticed Kamil was gone. My mind wandered to what Mykell and MJ told me.

I reached for my phone and called Mykell.

"Hello?" He sounded groggy.

Another contraction hit me and I yelled into the phone, "AHHH!"

"What's wrong? Neicey? Talk to me? You alright?" he asked never missing a beat.

"My water broke and I'm having contractions," I said breathing hard.

"Oh shit! You want me to meet you at the hospital?"

"No, I need you to take me. AHHH," I yelled again. "Kamil isn't here."

"I'm on my way."

Ten minutes later Mykell and MJ walked through the door. I guessed MJ used the key Kamil gave him. Mykell came to the bed to put some clothes on me while MJ grabbed the bags.

"This shit hurts like hell. Never... the... fuck... again," I said through gritted teeth.

Mykell laughed at me. "C'mon fat mama."

I swore Mykell did 100 all the way to the hospital. They immediately took me to a room. I was in labor for 12 hours before I could start to push. Mykell called everybody in the family. Mykell was the only allowed back in the room with me. "Okay Reneice, we need you to do one big push."

"UGHHHHH! Hurry up and get this boy out of me!" I knew Mykell's hand had to be hurting because I was squeezing the shit out of it. "Okay we see the head, one more big push and he'll come out."

I pushed with all my might until I heard my baby crying. I was crying right along with him, tears of pain and joy. "Okay, Dad, would you like to cut the umbilical cord?"

"Hell yeah!"

"Okay Reneice we need you to push one more time so we can get the afterbirth out of you." I pushed and all kinds of nasty stuff came out of me.

I was so tired I was fighting to keep my eyes open. Mykell brought Romell over to me. "Doc what's wrong with her? She doesn't look too good."

"She's fine; her body is tired because she just gave birth, so she just needs a little rest."

I knew he was scared because of what happened to his mother. "I'm fine," I gave him a weak but reassuring smile. I looked down at my handsome baby boy in my arms. He had a head full of hair, his father's chocolate complexion, and light brown eyes, but he had my dimples. He was the best thing that had ever happened to me. I was still a little upset that Kamil wasn't answering his phone, but Mykell was there and that was all that mattered.

"I know without a doubt that he's mine. No DNA test needed."

"Are you upset about Kya's baby?" I asked

"Hell naw, I knew when she was pregnant with her that she wasn't mine. It actually feels good."

"Aren't you going to go get the rest of the family?"

"Oh shit! Yeah, I'll be back."

A few minutes later, my room was filled with the people I loved, including my brother. We had put the past behind us and gotten back to the way we used to be.

"Aww he's almost as cute as me," MJ said and everybody laughed. "He has my eyes."

"Those would be *my* eyes," Mykell intervened.

"Actually, I think those eyes belong to me," Pop-Pop said setting them both straight.

"I guess he told y'all," I laughed.

"Can I hold my nephew now?" Lani asked

"Go ahead Auntie Lani," I said giving her Romell.

"Then pass him to Uncle Mack," Micah said.

"Then his *favorite* uncle wants to see him," Ramone joked.

"Aw, I just love y'all, all of you."

"Damn, me included?" Ramone asked with a smirk.

"Yes, asshole, you included."

At that moment Kamil walked in the room with a big teddy bear looking like he hadn't had a wink of sleep. "Sorry I'm late ma. I had business to take care of at the club and it took longer than I expected." He leaned over to give me a kiss. I caught some displeased looks from Mykell and Ramone. Mone was still salty with him for pulling a gun out on him. "It's cool, you're here now, and that's all that matters." My lips were saying one thing but I was feeling the complete opposite.

He walked over to Lani and looked at Romell. "All that hair explains why you had all that heartburn."

"I know. I'm just happy that it's over."

"Oh, Lisa called me when we were in the waiting room. I told her where we were at, and she wants to know if she can see the baby," Pop-Pop spoke up.

"Hell naw," Lani and I said at the same time.

"What the fuck Pops? You know I got rid of her, so ain't no need for her to be tryna see my son."

I didn't miss the emphasis he put on the word "my." Nigga, we know whose son he is. I just shook my head. That bitch had another thing coming if she thought she was going to have her ass around my son. Naw, she had the game fucked up.

Kya

9 months later

I heard that bitch had her baby. The killer part was Mykell didn't even get a damn DNA test done for her baby. My cousin wasted no time bragging about that shit. Fuck that, I was tired of that bitch living the life I was supposed to be living. They weren't even together anymore but he was still taking care of her and running after her ass. No worries though, all that shit was about to come to an end. My baby was one years old and he hadn't done shit for her since she was born. I knew he was mad that he found out she wasn't his, but what... the... fuck... ever! I had something for that ass.

Kya: It's time to put the plan in motion.

Unknown: I'm happy you finally decided to see things my way. Took you long enough.

Kya: Had to do some thinking and take care of my daughter.

Unknown: Yeah yeah yeah. Let's just get ready to fuck some shit up.

Kya: Ready when you are.

I just hoped that shit didn't come back to bite me in the ass.

Mykell

Thursday would be Neicey's 21st birthday. I decided that I would call her and see if she wanted me to get Romell so she could enjoy her day. "Talk to me," she said.

"Do you have to answer yo phone like that?" I joked.

"Yes I do," she giggled.

"What you doing?"

"Nothing, just feeding Fat Fat."

"Give him a kiss for me. I was calling to see if you wanted me to pick him up Thursday so you could go out and do girly stuff and damn near swipe the strip off my black card."

"Aren't you the sweetest, but that's cool with me. We were on our way over anyways because MJ got on my head about me not bringing his brother to see him."

"Aight, you know what to do." I was happy on the inside.

"Sure do, I'll be there in about 15 minutes."

"Cool, one."

Exactly 15 minutes later, Neicey walked through the door with Romell on her hip and a baby bag on her shoulder. She was looking delicious as hell. She had some short jean shorts and a corset top on. Thanks to Romell, her ass had gotten rounder, her hips spread a little, and she got thicker overall. I couldn't take my eyes of her. "Are you gonna drool over my lil sexy ass or are you going to speak and help me with this boy?"

"Shit, I'ma do both," I half joked. "What I tell you about bringing bags over here anyways? You know I've got everything he needs," I said while grabbing my son.

"I know, but I'm so used to taking a baby bag everywhere I go," she sighed while sitting down on the couch.

"Mell, what the hell yo mama been feeding you?" He smiled as if he understood what I was talking about. "Can you say Dada?"

He looked at me funny then smiled a toothless smile, "Mama," he said while clapping his hands. "That's mama's Fat Man!" She leaned over and kissed his cheek.

"Lil man, you turning on me?" I laughed before putting him in his playpen.

"Where's MJ's lil grown butt?" She asked giving Romell toys to play with. She backed up to sit back down on the couch and that was when I made my move. I pulled her on my lap and kissed her neck. "He's with Pops."

"Stop, Mykell, I told you I'm not going there with you no more," she said trying to get up.

Neicey and I had slept together two more times since that incident at the hotel. After she had Romell, I couldn't help myself, I had to have her. I didn't know why we always had to go through that. She knew she wanted it, so why fight it? I tried to unbutton her shorts, but she stopped me. "No, Mykell."

I just sighed. "Alright man."

"You know what you're doing tomorrow? You're about to be 26, old man," she said, still sitting on my lap.

"If I had it my way, I would be doing you tomorrow." I rubbed my hand up and down her thigh.

"Nasty ass."

"You like it yo, but I do know what I wanna do."

"What?"

"Spend time with you and my sons, as a family. Just us four."

She thought about it for a minute. "Okay," she shrugged.

"Good now…'

I was about to say something but my phone rang; it was Micah. "Wassup Macaroni?" I joked around with my older brother.

"Tryna see if you wanna roll with me to the surprise party Friday or should I say Thursday night?"

"Whose is it?" I asked as I watched Neicey take our son out of the playpen and play with him on the floor.

"Uhh Neicey," he said that like I should have already known.

"Well, I ain't know nothing about it."

"Now you do, so you going or what?"

"Yeah, I'll roll with you."

"Cool, I'll pick you up. It's an all-white party with a touch of purple since that's her favorite color," he informed me.

"Aight, but who giving it?"

"Her man," he chuckled.

"Aight man."

"Aight, one."

"One."

I watched as Neicey stood Romell up on his feet and faced him towards me. "Walk to Daddy Fat Fat," she said coaxing him. "He's been tryna walk for about a week now, but he just falls on his butt or sits down," she said.

He hesitated for a while, but he took a step. Neicey gasped and I sat up on the couch and spread my arms out tryna get him to come all the way. He looked at me and smiled before walking the rest of the way. Things like that were what made me proud to be a father. I missed some of those things with MJ because a few months after he was born, I was locked up. "See Fat Fat, I knew you could do it." Neicey beamed as she sat down on the couch with us.

"See, I should be able to experience this sit all the time instead of some other nigga!" My voiced filled with more anger than I expected it to, but shit, that's how I felt. She just put her head down. Romell looked at her; he must have known something was wrong with her. "Mama," he said touching her face. She looked at him and kissed his hand. "Mama is fine baby. You stay here with Daddy while I go to the bathroom." She got up and headed towards the back.

As soon as she closed the door, her phone rang. I wasn't going to answer it, but curiosity got the best of me and I noticed it was Kamil. "Hello?"

"Who the fuck is this?"

"Who the fuck you think?" I matched his attitude.

"Where my girl at?"

"She's kind of busy."

"I don't give a fuck how busy she is, put her on the phone!"

I chuckled. "You know I ain't going nowhere right?" I took the phone away from my ear because I didn't want to hear his bullshit. "Neicey, yo phone," I yelled.

"Who is it?"

"Yo prison guard."

She took the phone. "Hello?" She looked at me then went back in the back. I just sat there and smiled. I knew he felt some type of way about me answering her phone but oh well. He needed to be thanking me for letting him borrow her for that long. No worries though, when I told her ass to come, that was exactly what she was going to do. I still had her heart and they both knew that. I wondered how he would feel if he knew I still tasted the pussy. His ass thought he was doing something by not inviting me to her party. *Fuck that bitch ass nigga. She still my girl, always will be.*

Reneice

It was the morning of my birthday and I was supposed to be sleeping peacefully, but that was not happening. I heard arguing downstairs. I looked over at the clock and it was only 8:15 in the morning. I headed downstairs to see what all the commotion was about. I got down the stairs and saw Mykell standing there mad as hell. "What's wrong and why are y'all so loud?"

"This nigga tryna tell me I can't get my own son! Last time I checked, I was the one who busted that nut in you and got you pregnant, not him."

"Okay, that's enough." I turned to Kamil, "Wassup? Why you won't let him get Fat Fat?"

"The question is why you down here dressed like that?" I looked down at what I had on. I was dressed in some boy shorts and a tank top, the same thing I always wore to bed. "Uhh, I always wear this to bed, so why you tripping?"

"Because he doesn't want me to see all that, but what he fails to remember is that I've been all up in that plenty of times. Hell, I was the first person to ever hit it," Mykell smirked.

"Do me a favor and shut up," I fussed. I heard Romell crying. "Can you two please act like y'all got some sense while I check on my son? Please?" I went upstairs and changed Romell's diaper and then got him dressed. I didn't pack a bag since Mykell hated when I did. I went back downstairs with my son on my hip. Romell saw his dad and got happy, "Dada!" I stopped and looked at my baby, "Traitor," I laughed.

"That's what I'm talking about lil man, you finally got it right." He smiled like a proud father. "Oh, Lani said you better be ready when she comes to get you."

"Alright."

He turned to leave out the door. I looked over at Kamil and he was just staring at me. "Y'all need to cut all that bickering out, it is so unnecessary."

"That's that nigga, coming up in here like he runs shit."

"Aw, big baby." I said kissing his lips.

"You better go on before you start something you can't finish." He laughed.

* * *

After a long day of being pampered with Lani, I was relaxed. I missed my baby so I called to check on him while I was on my way home. "Yo," Mykell answered the phone.

"What's my baby doing?"

"I'm chilling, just watching TV."

I chuckled. "I was talking about Romell, asshole."

"Oh he's asleep. Its 10:00. What do you expect him to be doing, smart one?"

"I miss him, give him a kiss for me," I pouted.

"Alright where's mine though."

"Muah! Love ya baby daddy." I laughed.

"Yeah, yeah, yeah, love you too, knucklehead."

I hung up with Mykell as I was pulling in the driveway. I walked in the house not really ready to end my night. "Bae, where you at?"

"Upstairs, come here," he yelled.

I went upstairs to find Kamil dressed in an all-white Armani suit with the first three buttons of his dress shirt open and purple Stacy Adams. "Damn," was all I could say.

He turned and looked at me. "Hurry up and get dressed, we've got somewhere to be."

I looked in the garment bag on the bed, and saw a purple tight fitting crop top shirt, and a white long double slit skirt. I looked at him suspiciously wondering what he had up his sleeve. "Oh, the shoes are under the bed." He smirked before walking out of the room. "Don't keep me waiting too long."

I looked under the bed and pulled the shoebox from under it. There were some purple peep-toe high-heeled booties in there that matched my shirt perfectly. I got dressed and combed my new burgundy hair that was bone straight down my back and parted down the middle. When I was pregnant with Romell, my hair grew like mad.

After I was ready, I went downstairs. Kamil was waiting on me with a small box in his hand with a purple ribbon. "About time," he joked.

"You can't rush perfection boy, you know that."

"Your thighs look too damn juicy; I might have to make you change clothes."

"Whatever, so can I get my present now?"

"How you know this is for you?"

"Because I know, now come on," I squealed anxiously.

He laughed and pulled out a beautiful tennis bracelet and put it on my wrist. I was in awe. "Happy 21st birthday baby," he said kissing me.

"Thank you!"

"Alright, come on."

We went outside and got in his Navigator. I sat back and enjoyed the ride, asking no questions. We pulled up to his club. "C'mon baby, I've got something I need to check on real quick and I need you to come with me. I don't feel safe leaving you out here by yourself."

That was the first time I had been back there since I was raped. It had been a while. I took his hand and we walked through the entrance. "Mil Mil, it's too dark. You know I can't see." Right when I said that, the light came on. "Surprise!" I stood there shocked as hell. Surprised I was. I really wasn't expecting that. I looked over at Kamil and he had a big smile on his face. "You set me up," I laughed.

"Happy birthday, Mami," Lani yelled coming towards me. "You knew this the whole time I was with you today." She laughed at my pouty face, "Of course I did."

We made our way to the VIP section. "I wanna give a shout out to the birthday girl, Neicey. You looking real fly tonight boo," the DJ said. I looked over to his booth and blew him a kiss. I saw my brothers and Mykell chilling at one of the tables. "Happy birthday, Ladybug," Ramone stood to give me a hug. He looked at my outfit and his eyes damn near popped out of his head. "Where the fuck are the rest of your clothes?"

I just laughed at him, "Chill Mone, I'm 21 now. Let me enjoy my night and you can chew me a new asshole tomorrow."

"Happy birthday, knucklehead," Micah said giving me a hug also. "I got yo present out in the car."

"Thanks Mack."

Mykell licked his lips and gave me a hug, taking that as an opportunity to catch a free feel. "I love you and happy birthday," he whispered in my ear, lightly kissing it. I felt a tingle go through my body. I blushed and thanked him. The DJ started playing "Twerk It" by Busta and Lani and I gave each other that look. We headed straight for the dance floor. We moved our bodies to the beat of the music like we were at home in the mirror. When Nicki's part came on, I lost my mind. I loved Nicki's exotic ass. I felt all eyes on me but I didn't give a damn. It was my night and I wasn't about to let anyone kill my vibe.

Kya

I sat in the corner in the back of the club watching that bitch act like she owned the place. She was on the dance floor like she had no worries in the world. Too bad she didn't know what was about to hit her ass. I saw Mykell up in VIP drooling over her ass like she was all that or some shit. I'd let her enjoy her time for a little while longer. Then it was time to stir some shit up.

Reneice

To say I was having the time of my life would be an understatement. I really wasn't much of a drinker, but I had just turned 21, so why the hell not? I went to the bar and saw Johnny. He reached over the bar and hugged me. "Long time no see, baby girl, happy birthday by the way."

"Thanks, Johnny," I smiled. "Can I get some Peach Ciroc, please?"

"Anything for you, baby girl."

While I waited for my drink, I felt a presence behind me and already knew who it was. I knew his scent anywhere. "Having fun?"

I turned around and smiled at Mykell. I was about to respond before his new tattoo caught my eye. I was my name in big bold letters on his chest. I saw it through his white V-neck. "Oh my gosh Kell! When did you get this?"

"Earlier today. I got it for your birthday. It's not the whole thing, and it's not finished." I was taken aback, it was gorgeous, and I was shocked he did it. "It's beautiful."

"I'm glad you like it." He smiled. "You owe me a dance."

I was about to say something when Kamil came on the mic. "I wanna thank everybody for coming out and showing my lady some love on her birthday. We've got about 15 minutes before 12:00 but that don't mean the party is over. That just means I need to hurry up and give her the last present. Baby, come here."

I walked to the DJ booth and the spotlight hit us. "Baby, I just want to tell you how much I love you and how happy you make me. I remember the first time I laid eyes on you, it was your birthday, and you were working at Hooters. That day I knew you were something special, but you wouldn't give a nigga no play and kept my ass in the friend zone," he laughed and so did the crowd. "But fate finally brought us together and I'm the luckiest man on earth. All I wanna know is, will you marry me?" He got down on his knee and opened a ring box. My jaw hit the floor. It was the most beautiful ring I'd ever seen; besides the one Mykell gave me.

I had tears flowing from my eyes. "YES," I yelled. He stood up and I jumped in his arms hugging him tightly. That was the best birthday ever. "Promise" by Jagged Edge came on and he led me to the dance floor. I felt like I was floating on cloud nine. "This night can't get any better." We danced through "Let's Get Married," "Sure Thing," and when "Must Be Nice" came on; Mykell tapped Kamil on the shoulder. "Can I steal a dance with the birthday girl real quick?" he asked. Kamil said yeah without hesitation.

"You remember this used to be our song?"

"How could I forget? You used to sing this to me all the time."

"Yeah, I just wish I would have listened to Lyfe. Then maybe I would still have you."

I looked up in his eyes and I could see he was hurt. "You know Kell, I will always love you. You've given me one of the most precious gifts I've ever had in my life. This doesn't change how I feel about you," I spoke from the heart.

"I know, because it damn sure doesn't change how I feel about you either."

The rest of the dance was a quiet one until somebody pushed Mykell roughly from behind. He turned around and it was Lisa. *Well, well, well, so we meet again.* I thought to myself. "Look at what the trash brought in," I said.

"The fuck you putting yo hands on me for?" Mykell asked clearly pissed.

"Because I'm tired of you thinking the world of this bitch when she was the one who left yo dumb ass and you still running behind her ass like a lost puppy even though she clearly just got engaged to another nigga."

"Look hoe, I'm not gonna be too many more bitches."

Like always, Lani and I were in tune with each other. She came out of nowhere and stood by me ready to go to war. "Maybe if yo dry pussy ass was more like her, you could keep a man. I ain't seen or spoke to yo ass in over a year and you wanna pop off on some bullshit? Fuck outta here with that shit."

She slapped the shit out of Mykell. That was when Le'Lani and I pounced on her ass. That bitch was screaming trying to get us off her, but it was to no avail. We were beating that hoe like we should have done a long time ago. "I told yo stupid ass I wasn't gonna be pregnant forever hoe!"

Mykell grabbed me and Kamil grabbed Lani. Kamil led the way to his office with Micah and Ramone right on our heels. Kamil shut the door after Ramone walked in. Everyone was silent. "How my hair look?" I asked. "You look fine mami," Lani answered me.

"Good. You straight too, boo."

"That's all I need to hear."

"Are y'all serious right now?" Kamil asked.

"What?" Lani and I asked simultaneously as if we didn't know what he was talking about.

"You know what!"

"Uhn uhn, lower that tone."

"Y'all crazy," Micah laughed.

"Mack you already know how we do," I said.

"Yeah I do, we all do. But clearly your *fiancé* doesn't," he said.

"What do you mean?" Kamil asked.

"He means yo girl is a damn ticking time bomb and her best friend ain't no different. They been whooping ass together since they've known each other," Ramone spoke.

"Hell, that's how they met. Some hoes were on some tough shit with Lani and Neicey came to her defense. They didn't even know each other at the time," Ramone continued.

"Damn, really?"

Kell, remember yo first night, home?" Micah laughed.

"Let's not go there, Mack," I told him.

"Why not? You beat two people's ass that night. Then turned around and asked me if I thought you were crazy," Mykell spoke for the first time.

Kamil looked at him and for the first time he noticed his tattoo. I saw Kamil tense up, so I tried to defuse the problem before it even started. "Whatever, I'm not that bad."

"Ladybug, you remember what happened when you were nine. I knew then that yo ass was a hot head."

"But that's different." I put my head down remembering that horrible occasion.

"Why didn't you ever tell us about that?" Mykell asked.

"You know?" I asked surprised.

"I told him," Ramone said.

"What happened?" Kamil asked confused about what we were talking about.

"Nothing, I don't wanna think about it anymore."

"Cool."

The change of tone in his voice didn't go unnoticed, well not by me at least. I also noticed he looked at me funny. "Neicey, come here. Let me holla at you real quick," he said, walking to the bathroom.

I already knew what he wanted to talk about, but I went anyways.

"You think that was some cute shit you just pulled out there? Huh?" he asked walking up on me.

"Kamil, what the fuck is you talking about?" I asked playing dumb.

"You know what the fuck I'm talking about. Out there fighting in the damn club like you some type of rat bitch or something."

I was a little taken aback because he had never spoken to me like that before.

"Look Kamil, you got the shit twisted. Especially if you think I'm not going to protect myself."

"That's just it Reneice. You weren't fighting for you; you were fighting for that nigga out there. Not even an hour after I proposed to yo ass. What, this don't mean shit to you?" he asked taking my hand with the ring on it.

"Kamil, you tripping and you better fix that damn attitude. I don't know what's wrong with you tonight, but let's not have this lil episode ever again," I said walking out of the bathroom. *I know he was feeling some type of way, but damn.*

Kamil

I was still pissed off about the shit that happened that night. She claimed she didn't want the nigga but for some reason I still felt like I had to compete with his ass. *Fuck that. I put too much time in for him to come back in and think he's gonna take her back.*

My thoughts were broken by Neicey's scream. I looked at her like she was crazy. "MY CAR," she screamed again. I looked out the passenger side window and saw what she was having a fit about. "Damn!" *Her shit is fucked.* All the windows were busted out, her tires were flat, and it had dents in it everywhere. Somebody had spray painted the word "bitch" on the hood and trunk. She went and took a piece of paper from under the wiper. She read it and threw it on the ground. "What the fuck?" she yelled on the verge of tears.

I picked up the paper and read, "*You better watch your back you dumb bitch.*" It was signed *xoxo* at the bottom. "I'ma kill that bitch," she fumed, walking towards the front door. I had a gut feeling who was behind it, but I wasn't going to say anything until I knew for sure. "Who do you think did it?" I asked.

"It had to be Lisa's bitch ass!" I was almost positive I knew who it was, and I didn't think it was Lisa. "Baby, just go lay down and get some rest. It's almost 4:00 in the morning. We'll figure this out in the morning and I'll take you to get a new car."

She sighed, "Alright, Kamil."

Truth was, I was happy the car was trashed. That was the same car that Mykell had gotten her for Christmas when they were together. I had been trying to get her a new car for the longest, but she'd refused. Now she had no choice. She should have just done it in the first place. I pulled my phone out of my pocket and sent a text.

Kamil: I need to talk to you about some shit. I'll be there in the morning so be ready.

I turned my phone off without waiting for a response. I headed upstairs to be with my lady, or should I say my fiancé. I'd noticed the tattoo that Mykell had on his chest and wondered why the fuck he would do some shit like that. I bet he felt stupid as fuck for getting it after I proposed. Oh well, his loss, my gain. My next step was to knock her ass up with a lil Kamil Jr. and really make his ass sick.

*   *   *

I woke up the next morning on a mission. I had some business to handle. I pulled up to the hood with one thing on my mind. I knocked on the door and waited for somebody to answer it. It opened and I went in. "Did you pull that bullshit last night?"

"I don't know what you're talking about."

"I bet you do. Let me find out you did that shit to my girl's car and that's yo ass. I really don't give a fuck about the car. I don't appreciate you thinking it's okay to fuck with her. Leave her alone and I'm not asking." I pulled up my shirt to show the butt of my .45 just to show how serious I was. "Fuck with me if you want to and you'll regret it," I said before walking out the door.

Chapter 4

Mykell

Micah and I were riding through the hood a few weeks earlier when we saw something real suspicious. Neicey's boy toy Kamil was coming out of a house that wasn't meant for anything good. I should know because I had been there a couple of times myself. I wanted to call Neicey up right then and there, but Micah didn't think it was a good idea. He told me to check into it first before I brought it to her.

I decided to bring in somebody who didn't like his ass as much as I didn't, Ramone. He was the perfect person because that was his baby sister and he still had a personal vendetta against him for the gun incident. So, I decided to pay him a visit.

"Wassup, knucklehead, where ya man at?" I asked my sister when she opened the door.

"In the kitchen, of course." I headed to the kitchen and that nigga was cooking something that smelled good as fuck. "Hurry up, Chef Boyar*negro*? I've got some real shit to holla at you about."

"Well, don't keep an asshole in suspense. Tell me now."

I told him what I saw and he was not happy. "So either this nigga in an undercover crackhead or he's playing my sister?"

"Pretty much."

"You told her yet?"

"Nah, Mack told me to do some digging before I brought it to her, so that's exactly what I'ma do."

"You know we can't let her marry this nigga, right? There's just something about that nigga that I don't trust and that info ain't makes it no better. I don't want his ass around my sister or nephew."

"I know man. Ever since she got engaged to that nigga, she's been acting all funny. I used to talk to her and see my son damn near every day. I'm lucky if I see him once a week now."

"Translation, since he popped the question you ain't be getting none no more," he laughed.

"Nigga how you know?"

"C'mon man that's my little sister, she told me. She asked me if she should feel bad and I told her naw. She knows that you still have her heart; she also told me that she loved the nigga but she's not all the way in love with him. She thinks there's something holding her back from loving him completely."

"So she's not in love with him because she still loves me?"

"Correction, she's still in love with you," Lani said coming into the kitchen.

"What's the difference Le'Lani?"

"She loves him because when you were on your bullshit, he was there for her. He spent time with her, he would comfort her, he was the first person that she told when she found out she was pregnant the first time. He was basically a shoulder for her to cry on when she couldn't talk to you or us, and eventually he became a dick for her to ride on because you let that happen. But she doesn't think that everything he does is sincere. She thinks he's just trying to compete with you. He's been pressuring her lately about having a baby, but little does he know; she got the IUD so she won't be having kids for 5 years unless she gets it taken out."

"Damn, see, even I didn't know all of that," Ramone said shaking his head.

"Yup, it's a girl thing; she even said he flipped about that tattoo you got. He was happy when her car got fucked up; only because that was the car you bought her," she said pointing at me.

"Somebody messed up her car?" I asked just then finding that out.

"Yup, she thinks it was Lisa, but I don't think so. Lisa doesn't know where Kamil lives," she said before leaving the kitchen.

She had just left me with some heavy shit on my mind. She and Ramone both put some heavy shit on my mind. I was happy to know that she was still in love with a nigga, and that gave me a little hope that I could get my lady back. It was crazy that nigga was jealous of me, what for though. He wanted her, now he got her, so why he still worried about me. All bullshit aside though, it was time for me to get my family back.

Ramone

My sister had been acting really distant since she accepted that fuck boy's proposal. I didn't approve of it, but that was Ladybug's life, not mine. She was old enough to make her own mistakes and the only thing I could do was be there to catch her when she fell and bumped her head. I had a shocking visitor pop up on my doorstep a few days ago. I was confused about what to do so Lani told me to holla at Pops about it. That was exactly what I did. He called Ladybug and told her to come over to his house and bring baby Mell.

"Pops, do you really think this is going to work?" I asked nervously.

"I don't know, son, we just have to wait and see."

"I know, but you remember what I told her, what if she flips out. You know how her temper is."

"No worries, she always listens to me."

Ever since the day Pops put me on my ass for hitting Reneice, I hadn't taken a drink since. I took that ass whooping as a lesson learned. He was the one who helped me realize I didn't need to be drinking if I was going to be flipping out all the time.

"Pops, I think me and Ladybug need to go see a therapist. We have too many issues that have gone undealt with for too long," I voiced my concerns.

"That sounds good to me, I'm sure she'll go if you do."

"Pop-Pop," she yelled.

"Come in the den!"

She walked in with my handsome nephew right behind her. "Hey Fat Man." He walked over to Pops and me.

"What're you doing here bighead?"

"I have a surprise for you and I need to talk to you about something," I said looking at her.

"Uh oh, what I do now?"

"Yo ass been MIA, but we'll talk about that later."

Right when I said that, the doorbell rang. I looked over at Pops and he nodded his head. I got up to answer the door and was standing face to face with an older version of me. "Wassup, Dad?"

"Nothing much man, just taking it day by day."

"Well c'mon in, she's already here."

We walked back into the den and Neicey was taking out toys for Romell to play with while he sat in Pops' lap. "Ladybug," she turned around and noticed our dad. She looked at him funny then she gasped. "Oh my God! You guys look like twins!"

"Ladybug, this is our father, Ramone Senior."

"Father? Senior? What the hell?" She was clearly confused.

"Yeah, I'm a junior," I chuckled.

"I never knew that. Well what is he doing here?"

"I came to see you," our dad told her.

"Mone, I thought you said that he didn't want anything to do with me when he found out Mama was pregnant with me," she said looking at me with her hands on her hips.

"Uhh, I, well." All eyes were on me. I was nervous as hell.

"Well Reneice, that's not true. In fact, I was ecstatic when I found out Joyce was pregnant again, especially when I found out you were a girl. I did some bad things that caused me to go do a lengthy bid, so I went away before you were even born. I was the one who named you and everything. I beat myself up for not being there for you or Mone. When I got out, I went to Grand Rapids to look for you but I was informed that you had moved. It took me a while to track y'all down, but I did."

"So you didn't run out on Mama because you didn't want me?"

"Not at all."

She walked over to me and punched me in the chest. "Jerk, why you lie to me? You had me thinking I was the reason I didn't have a father."

"I'm sorry Ladybug, I was drunk."

"That's no excuse," she chastised me.

"Mama, juice," Romell said.

She walked over to Romell and picked him up off Pops' lap. "Romell, this is your grandpa. Say hi." He looked at him for a minute then smiled and reached for him. "He likes you."

My dad, I mean our dad, held Romell in his arms, and smiled. "How old is he?"

"He'll be one next month." She smiled proudly.

"Wow, my son's 29, my daughter's 21, and I have a grandson that's about to be one. Y'all make me feel old."

I was happy that Ladybug took that well and accepted him. I just knew she was going to act an ass when she found out, but she shocked the hell outta me. My next step was to get her to go to therapy with me.

Reneice

I was so happy about my reunion with my dad. All those years, I thought he was a deadbeat and was so angry with him. Now I knew I was mad for nothing. I remember not one time did my mom bad talk him, dog him out, or any of that stuff. She sure wouldn't allow us to do it and now I knew why. I wished I would have known that sooner. *Better late than never.* I'd been spending a lot of time with him since we met. I guess you could call it making up for lost time.

"So Dad, why did you leave us?" I asked trying to figure out where he was all my life.

"I had got into some legal issues."

"Like what?" I asked, wanting him to go more in depth.

"I went to prison for murder. I took a plea for 18 years and that's what I got, but I also had to do an extra two years for the firearm."

"Wow, who did you kill and why?"

He was silent for a minute. "I killed a man for putting his hands on your mother."

I could tell that it was a touchy subject for him so I left it alone.

"You really loved her didn't you?" I asked referring to my mom.

"Hell yeah, she was my first love. I would've done anything for her, which is why I got locked up and if I had to do it all over again, I would still kill him."

I could see the love in his eyes when he said that. "I want that one day," I said.

"What?"

"Somebody who loves me unconditionally and that would do anything for me."

"What happened with you and Romell's father?"

"He just couldn't seem to be faithful. Hell, when he was trying to get with me, he already had a girlfriend that I didn't know about. I know I should have taken that as a sign to leave him alone, but I fell for him anyways, no matter how hard I tried to fight it."

"Do you still love him?" he asked.

"Honestly, yes I do, but I don't think I'm in love with him anymore. It just feels different now."

"Do you love your boyfriend you're with now?"

I had to think about that one for a minute. *Do I love Kamil?*

"I mean yeah, I guess. He was there for me when I needed him the most and he was always a really good friend."

"Do you feel obligated to be with him?"

"No, I'm with him because I want to be with him."

"Or are you with him just to forget about Mykell?" he asked.

I got quiet. I really didn't know how to answer that, or if I even wanted to answer that. Maybe I was with Kamil to keep my mind off Mykell. I really did like Kamil, but sometimes I wondered if I jumped in a relationship with him too fast. Especially after everything that happened with Mykell.

My dad and Romell got along perfectly fine. I guess he was enjoying being around him since he never got to do it with me and his time was cut short with Ramone. "So. How does your boyfriend, I mean fiancé feel about Romell and when am I going to meet his father?" he asked out of the blue. It kind of threw me off because I wasn't expecting that. "Well Kamil is fine with Fat Fat, he doesn't treat him any different, and he already knows if he wants to be with me, he has to accept my son. It's not a problem for him."

"And his father?"

"He's very active in his life. He spends time with him and he does stuff for him. But lately, he hasn't seen him as much because we've become distant since I got engaged."

"When can I meet him? Mone already gave his approval but I would love to meet my grandson's father."

I thought, *what harm could it do?* "You can meet him now if you would like."

"Sure, why not," he said playing with Romell. I took out my phone and dialed Mykell's number. I didn't know why, but for some reason I was nervous. "Wassup?" he answered sounding like I was bothering him.

"You busy?" I was hoping he would say yes.

"Naw, me and MJ just woke up from a nap.

"Well Fat Fat and I are on the way, I have somebody I want you to meet."

"Well come through."

"Okay."

I looked at my dad and noticed how handsome he was. Prison makes some people look old but it didn't age him a bit. "You ready?"

"Yeah, let's go."

I hadn't seen Mykell in three weeks, since the night of my birthday. I was avoiding him because I wanted the relationship with Kamil to work. I didn't want Mykell getting in the way of me being happy. Yeah, Kamil and I had some issues we had to work out but what relationship didn't?

We pulled up to Mykell's house. I got a nervous feeling in my stomach and I wished it would go away. I grabbed Fat Fat from the backseat, and all three of us headed for the front door. I took out my key and unlocked the door. "Oh it's like that?" my dad chuckled.

"It's not what you think." I shook my head.

I put my son down and opened the door. He took off running the moment it opened. "Daddy," he ran for his father.

"Wassup lil man." He pulled his son on his lap.

I cleared my throat and he looked up at me and then at my dad. "Mykell, this is my dad Ramone Sr., Dad, this is Mykell, Romell's father."

Mykell stood up and shook his hand. "Nice to meet you sir."

"Likewise, I've wanted to meet you since I found out about my grandson."

"Oh yeah?" Mykell looked over at me and I looked away.

"MJ! Come here." I tried to avoid the confrontation I knew was coming. MJ came running down the stairs and right into me, hugging me tight. "Hi Mom! Long time no see, but it's okay. I forgive you."

I chuckled because he was just too grown. "I want you to meet my Dad, knucklehead. Dad, this is Mykell Jr., MJ, this is my dad."

"Ohhhh! So you're like my grandpa?"

He smiled, "I think so lil man."

"Um, Neicey can I holla at you real quick?" Mykell asked.

"Sure you can. I will stay here with my grandsons," my dad said before I could answer. I just looked at him. "Gon' head girl," he urged me.

I sighed because I already knew where that was going. I had been trying to avoid all that, but I supposed it didn't work.

We walked to the back bedroom. "Wassup?" I asked.

"Can you at least shut the door?" he asked. I stood there with my arms folded.

He sighed and walked over to the door and closed it. "What's yo problem?"

"What makes you think I have a problem?" I got defensive.

"Maybe because I haven't gotten to spend any time with my son since you decided to play the loving housewife."

"Are you mad because you haven't seen your son or because you haven't been able to get in my panties?" I asked with an attitude.

He chuckled, but I didn't see shit funny. "Baby girl, please, yo pussy is the furthest thing from my mind. I ain't never had a problem getting it from you or anybody else, so stop acting like you're the only one walking around with one. Now as far as my son goes, that lil bullshit you on keeping him from me; it ends today. I don't give a fuck if you marry the fucking Prince of England, I better be able to get my son. Or that's yo ass, now play with me if you want to."

We stood there in a staring match for a few minutes. I was shocked that he had just said that shit to me. Maybe he was finally moving on and realizing that we were over. That was exactly what I wanted, or was it?

Chapter 5

Kamil

It was Romell's first birthday. Neicey was driving herself crazy making sure everything was in order. She decided to have the party over at her Pop Pop's house. We weren't expecting anybody but family because Neicey's lil mean ass didn't like anyone. It was going to be a family get together and birthday party. I really wasn't in the mood to be around her bitch ass baby daddy, but it wasn't about him. It was about lil man. If he did step out of line, I had no problem putting that nigga in his place. There was no sense in acting like a bitch when he lost her fair and square. If he would have been doing right from jump, she wouldn't have come to me. In the words of Drake, "I know he messed up but let a real nigga make it right."

"Neicey, chill ma. You gonna drive yo lil self crazy," I said.

She sighed. "I know Kamil, but I just want everything to be perfect. I just can't believe my baby is one year old already. It feels like I just had him."

"I know. Before you know it me and lil man will be out riding around picking up girls," I laughed but it was cut short when Neicey punched me in the chest.

No lie that shit hurt like hell. Her lil ass could pack a mean punch.

"I was just playing baby, damn," I said rubbing my chest.

"Yeah well you play too much," she said pouting.

"Awww, my baby mad?" I asked pulling her close to me.

"Move Kamil," she laughed.

"Give me a kiss and I'll move."

"C'mon Kamil, I have to finish getting stuff ready for the party."

"Give me a kiss."

"No," she said trying to move.

I grabbed her by her waist and pulled her closer to me. She finally gave in and gave me a passionate kiss. After what seemed like forever, she broke the kiss. "That's what I'm talking about." I laughed.

Ramone

I knew its little man's birthday, but I had a surprise for Neicey also. She done got up here in the D and forgot about her brothers back home. I called to let them know that their nephew was having his very first birthday and they said they would be there. I asked Pops if it was cool and he said no problem. I couldn't wait to see the look on her face. After my mom passed, my homeboys helped me look after Neicey. There were five of us total. Me, Corey, Jason, Howie and Lakey. With Lakey only being two years older than Neicey, they were always together. They didn't think we knew but I knew they had something going on together. I knew she would be shocked to see them.

"Damn Lani, did you have to buy all these toys?" I asked putting all Romell's gifts in the car.

"Yes I did, I mean my nephew only turns one once."

"He probably won't even play with all these toys," I joked.

"Of course he will, now shut up and hurry up," she fussed.

"If you wouldn't have bought every toy in the store, we could have been there twenty minutes ago."

"Whatever," she rolled her eyes.

"I'm gonna hate to see how you act when we get kids of our own," I said putting the last two gifts in the car.

"Well, don't wait on it."

"Why every time I bring up the subject about us having kids, you always cop a damn attitude?"

"I don't have a damn attitude Ramone."

"Well I can't tell Le'Lani," I said sarcastically. "What is it? You don't want to have kids with a nigga or something?"

"It's not that."

"Then what the hell is it then? Help me understand," I said getting mad.

"I'm scared okay," she yelled. "I fucking lost my mother because she gave birth to me and I don't want to end up like her and miss out on my child's life."

Damn. Now I felt like shit. "I'm sorry baby, I didn't know. I understand how you feel. I don't want you to feel like I'm pressuring you into having a baby. We can wait till you're ready, if you ever become ready," I said.

I knew it had to be hard for her. I never thought about that, she had a legit reason to be scared. It would be nice to have some little ones running around, but I was not about to force her to do anything she was not ready to do.

The rest of the ride to Pops' house was quiet. I really felt bad about getting on her earlier. I should have talked to her instead of jumping to conclusions.

"Baby, I'm sorry. I didn't mean to get mad at you earlier." I said

She turned and looked at me. "It's fine, Ramone. I understand where you're coming from, but I also need you to understand where I'm coming from. I want to have kids someday, but I have some personal issues that I need to get over first." With that said, she got out of the car.

Chapter 6

Reneice

We were all in Pop-Pop's back yard chilling. MJ was running around playing with Romell, those two were inseparable. I would be lying if I said there wasn't some tension in the air though and it was pretty thick. Not only between Mykell and I, but Mykell and Kamil, and also Kamil and Ramone. Everyone was keeping calm and staying out of their feelings because it was Romell's day and I refused to mess it up. "Did I hear somebody say there was a party going on?" I stopped dead in my tracks. *It couldn't be, is it really?* I turned around and saw all four of my brother's friends.

"OH MY GODDDD," I screamed then ran to the closet one. I jumped in Corey's arms like I used to when I was little.

"What are you guys doing here?" I gave each one of them a hug.

"Well you got down here and neglected us, so we decided to come show out on you."

"Um, are you going to introduce us?" I heard Kamil say from behind me.

"Everybody, this is Corey, Jason, Howie, and Lakey." I pointed to each one of the men that helped Ramone raise me. I looked over at Lakey and started smiling from ear to ear. Lakey and Corey were brothers, but since Lakey was only two years older than me, we seemed to always get left together all the time. He was my first boyfriend. He was even my first love. He was so mad at me when I told him I was moving, but I had to do something with my life.

"Wassup, Ladybug, long time no see. You act like you don't even know a nigga no more." He smiled that gorgeous smile I loved so much.

"Whatever Lake, it ain't even like that."

"Yeah? Well how is it then?"

"Ugh, we'll talk later."

"Bet."

I could feel Kamil's eyes burning a hole in the side of my face. *He jealous, that's cute.* On the other hand, Mykell seemed to be cool. I didn't know why I was worried about how he felt anyways.

"So where's our nephew anyways?" Howie asked.

I turned to see MJ and Romell running around the backyard. *I love my boys.* "Fat Fat, come here," I called out to Romell. He turned, looked at me with a big smile on his face, and ran his little self towards me.

"Mama, play," he reached for me to pick him up.

"Mama will play with her baby in a minute; I want you to meet your uncles."

"Uncle?"

"Yes."

He looked at the four men standing in front of us. "Hi," he said shyly.

"Wassup lil man," Jason spoke. "I'm Uncle Jay, that's Howie, Corey, and Lakey."

Romell just smiled. "Play?" he asked Jason.

"Sure lil man, let's play."

I watched as Jason played with Romell and MJ. They were playing football. I felt so blessed to have those people in my life.

"Okay everybody, let's eat," Pop-Pop announced.

We sat at the big table that Pop-Pop had on his patio. "Uhh, I just know y'all about to go wash y'all hands?" Lani said with her hands on her hips.

"Well, excuse us," Ramone laughed.

I grabbed my Fat Man and put him on my lap. I loved my son more than anything in the world. I never thought I could love someone so much. I could say Mykell had given me the best thing in the world. Everyone came back from washing their hands so we blessed the food and dug right on in. I started to feed Romell but he shook his head. "I want Daddy," he said.

"You turning on me Fat Fat?" I asked faking hurt.

He kissed me on the lips and smiled with his two bottom teeth showing. I just laughed and took him over to Mykell. I gave him Fat Fat's plate. He tried to make eye contact with me but I kept ignoring him.

"So bighead, how do you like motherhood?" Corey asked.

"I love it! Fat Fat is my world." I smiled at my son.

"I remember when you were that little, we would all be chilling in Mone's room and you would just walk in there like you owned the room," he laughed.

"Yeah that's when we liked you," Howie joked

I rolled my eyes, "Whatever."

"He make you want some more?"

Before I even could speak, Kamil jumped in. "We're working on it."

I looked at Lani then Ramone. "Uhh, naw I don't want any more for a couple of years. Fat and MJ are enough for me right now," I spoke up

He looked at me crazy. "So what you saying?"

"I think I made it plain and clear what I was saying. I don't want any more kids for a few years."

He chuckled. "That's some bullshit."

"How you figure?"

"Because yo ass was quick to get pregnant by that nigga. Not once but twice. When I try to get you pregnant, yo ass is quick to get on birth control."

"Man," Ramone started to say, but I cut him off, "Naw Mone, I got this."

"Excuse you, but I went on birth control after I had Romell because what the fuck I look like being only 21 years old popping out babies back to back with no job because yo ass don't want me working? Make it make sense Kamil." I rolled my neck clearly getting pissed off.

"If that was the case, you would've got on birth control after you lost the first baby, but naw you laid on yo back and got knocked up again. I'm starting to think you just don't want to have my baby because I ain't that nigga!"

"Fuck you and this bullshit!" I was so mad I wanted to punch that nigga in his jaw for saying some shit like that. If I wasn't going to those damn therapy sessions with Ramone I would've went the fuck off. Instead, I just got up and walked into the house. I was so mad I had tears streaming down my face.

"Neicey," I heard Lani yell, but fuck that, I refused to stop or turn around. Here it was supposed to be my son's birthday and Kamil was trying to make shit about him. I didn't know where that attitude was coming from, nor did I give a damn. All of a sudden, he wanted to show out and throw a bitch fit. *Fuck him.*

Lakey

That was some crazy shit that just happened. I knew her nigga had some bitch in him when I first laid eyes on him. I didn't even know why she with his ass anyways. What the fuck could his scrawny ass do for her?

"Man let me go check on her," Ramone said pissed off.

"Naw Mone, I got this one," I said mugging her bitch of a nigga.

Shit, I had her before either of them two niggas out there did, but that was beside the point. I met her baby daddy a few days ago and he was cool. Of course,

I told him about mine and Ladybug's history. He was cool about it and said he wasn't on no beefing shit with me because I was before he came around. He expressed his concerns with me about her new nigga though. He and Ramone gave me the rundown on everything that had been happening. It broke my damn heart when I found out that my Snook was raped. That shit almost happed when she was 9 years old so I had taught her how to shoot a gun to protect herself.

I found her in the kitchen pacing back and forth. "Come here Snook."

She looked at me with tears in her eyes. She looked like the little girl I grew up with and fell in love with when I was 14 years old. "Fuck that nigga and the bullshit he talking. He can't force you to do something you don't want to do."

"I'm tired of everybody treating me like I'm in the wrong. Mykell's mad at me because I'm engaged to Kamil and won't take him back. Kamil's mad at me because I won't have his baby. I'm just tired of everything Lakey." She broke down crying.

"Hey now, you know how I feel about you and that crying shit. Wipe them eyes and cut all that shit out." I rubbed her back.

"I'm just tired, Lashaun," she called me by my government.

"I know, but you know I don't like you crying. You don't have to have that nigga's baby if you don't want to. Shit he don't even seem like yo type, so why are you with him?"

"What makes you think he's not my type?" she asked with her hands on her hips.

"Because he's not me," I chuckled

"Whatever Lakey."

"No but seriously, he's not your type because he's a light-skinned nigga. You've never been into them, you like chocolate, always have. Hell, look at me and yo baby daddy."

"Now you ain't lying," she laughed. "But he was there for me when Mykell and I were having problems. He would talk to me and help me make decisions. He would kick it with me when Mykell didn't have time for me," she shrugged.

"So basically you're with him because you got comfortable with him. He was plotting on yo relationship the whole time and you ain't een know," I said mocking Rocko.

She laughed. "I guess, but it's crazy because after I left Mykell, I went to his house and that's where I've been ever since. We never even really made it official."

"Like I said, you got comfortable with him. You feel like you have to be with him because he was a shoulder for you to cry on. Now look where that got you."

"I know," she sighed.

"So how about we say fuck him and you bring yo ass back home where you belong, with me," I stated.

"With you huh? It's not that simple Lakey."

"You still love him don't you?"

"Who?"

"Your son's father."

"Nope." She bit her lip. She always did that when she was lying or hiding something.

"As much as I don't appreciate you leaving me and giving that nigga everything that was supposed to be mine, I can tell you still love him. I can tell he loves you too."

"How do you know?"

"I had a conversation with him. I could tell by the way he talked about you and the look he had in his eyes at the mention of your name."

She looked down, "Lashaun, I'm sorry for just up and leaving you. I know it was wrong, but I had to do it to better my life. Coming here and falling in love and having a baby were never part of the plan, ever."

"It's cool Snook. I understand, this shit doesn't change how I feel about you. You will always be my Snook," I said walking up to her and raising her head. I leaned down and kissed her passionately, not giving a fuck about neither one of those niggas sitting out there.

"Oooh wee! I knew it, y'all niggas ain't slick."

We looked up to see Corey and Ramone standing there. "Shut up fool," Snook said.

"Well damn, it was two niggas now it's three. Ladybug what are you doing to these niggas?"

"Don't even play Mone. You know I was here way before any of them niggas. They should be thanking me for letting them borrow her. If they keep fucking up, she knows where to find me. Naw, but for real, talk to ya baby daddy. It looks like y'all have some unfinished business," I said before walking back outside.

Chapter 7

Mykell

I knew shit would hit the ceiling fan between them two sooner or later. It was supposed to be about my son but that bitch ass nigga found a way to make it about him and fuck it up. I just sat back not saying anything. I looked at that nigga and started laughing, he was really a bitch made ass nigga yo.

"Fuck is you laughing at?"

"Yo sweet ass," I spat. "You fucking up my son birthday and I don't appreciate that shit. I don't appreciate you upsetting the mother of my child, either."

"Nigga fuck you, whatever the fuck me and Neicey go through ain't got shit to do with you," he tried to get loud.

"It got everything to do with me when you sit in my face and upset her. It most definitely got shit to do with me when you put my name in it." I got up and put Romell in Lani's lap because I knew shit was about to get real.

"Nigga yo ass just mad because she don't want yo ass no more." He stood up acting tough. Ramone and Neicey walked out of the house.

I smirked, "Oh yeah? Well I can't tell because I've been up in that just as much as you have since y'all been together. Nigga I can get it whenever I want and that's been a proven fact."

I didn't mean to put Neicey out like that but I had to let that nigga know that he didn't have shit on me. "I know for a fact that she was faithful when she was with me but can you say the same?" I laughed. I saw Pops get up out of the corner of my eye, he was about to defuse the situation before it could get worse.

"Really Neicey? You been fucking this nigga behind my back? That's how we doing this shit now?" he asked when she got to us.

She shot me an evil look but I didn't give a damn. "It only happened three times and I haven't done it since you gave me the ring."

He laughed. "Nigga I don't give a fuck what y'all had, you need to face the fact that I have her now."

"Fuck ever nigga. You need to face the fact that I'll be around all the time and I ain't going nowhere, ever."

That nigga tried to run up on me and I caught him right in his jaw. He tried to come back, but I hit him with another two-piece. I heard Neicey yelling in the background and Mell screaming. I turned to look at my son then I heard a gun cocking. That bitch nigga had his gun pointed at me. I smirked when I heard about five other guns cocking. I looked and saw Ramone and his boys pointing their guns at Kamil. "Lani, take my sons in the house, now!"

She did as I told her. Pop-Pop came and stood by me. "Son put the gun down, all this ain't even necessary," he said.

"Yeah boy, put that gun down, you're outnumbered anyways," I taunted. I caught the dirty look Pops gave me but I was testing that nigga's gangster.

Neicey stood directly in front of his gun. "Is this what you really wanna do?"

"Reneice move the fuck out of the way, if that nigga shoot you I'm going back to prison," Ramone said.

"I got this y'all," she turned around and said.

She whispered something in that nigga's ear and he lowered his gun. "Put the guns away y'all," she told her brother and his friends. "And if anyone one of y'all ever pull a gun out around my sons, I've got a bullet for each and every one of you. Now try me if you want to."

I smirked because her lil ass was always threatening somebody. She turned and looked at me; she grabbed my arm and pulled me away from everybody. "You straight?" she asked.

"Yeah, I'm cool."

"Good," she punched me in the chest. No lie, that shit hurt.

"Fuck was that for man?" I asked while rubbing my chest.

"For running yo damn mouth. That shit was supposed to stay between us, why the fuck would you do that?"

"Man, that nigga was talking crazy and I had to put him in his place."

"What's his place Mykell? You just do shit to get under my skin," she fumed.

"His place is being a damn rebound nigga! And don't question me about shit I do, you know better."

"I can't fucking stand you!"

"I know something you can stand though," I smiled devilishly.

"Fuck you," she shook her head.

"If that's what you want then I can make that happen for you."

She just rolled her eyes. "Anyways, can you keep Fat tonight?"

"Do you gotta ask me to keep my son?"

"Just answer the question."

"Yeah, man, I got him."

"Thank you."

"That's not how I want to be thanked."

"Whatever Kell," she said, walking away. *Damn, that ass getting fat. It's really time for her to bring her ass home. I've had enough of this bullshit.*

Kamil

The ride home was a quiet one. I was pissed to find out that Neicey had fucked that nigga behind my back. Not one but three times. Shit, I couldn't be mad at her for keeping secrets seeing how I was keeping one myself. Something deep inside me wanted to tell her. *Fuck it, I'ma tell her.* I went upstairs to find her, when I got to the room I saw the whole room lit with candles and she was standing there in an all-black lace teddy. *She knows that's my favorite color.* She walked up to me, "I'm sorry about tonight, actually I'm sorry about everything. I promise you I haven't slept with him for months and it will *never* happen again. I don't want him. Here is where I wanna be."

I could even think straight because my dick was standing at attention. "It's cool; I know how to punish that ass."

She grabbed my hand and led me to the end of the bed where she had a chair waiting. She pushed me down in it and when to the stereo system. "Dance for You" by Beyoncé came on. She walked over to the stripper pole I had in our room and turned to look at me with lust in her eyes. *This shit about to get good.*

She climbed up the pole and hung upside down with her legs still wrapped around the pole. Then she came down into a full split. "Damn! Yo ass been holding out," I said, grabbing my dick. She walked over to me seductively and she straddled my lap and started grinding slowly while licking my neck. She started singing in my ear.

I wanna say thank you in case I don't thank you enough

A woman in the street and a freak in the you know what

Sit back, sit back. It's the pre-game show, daddy you know what's up

Loving you is really all that's on my mind.

I couldn't take it no more. The way she was grinding on my dick and licking my neck had me about to bust in my pants. I picked her lil ass up and carried her to the bed. I laid her down and slid her panties to the side, fuck taking them things off. I unbuckled my pants and let them fall to the ground, I didn't bother stepping out of them or taking my boxers off. My dick shot through the hole in my boxers and I did one big thrust into her wetness.

She was still grinding to the music, so I found her spot and pounded with no mercy. "Uhh! Mil wait!" She was trying to talk but I wasn't hearing shit. "Nope, I told you I was gonna punish yo ass," I said picking up speed,

"Turn yo ass over," I demanded and she did as she was told.

I continued pounding and grabbed a handful of her hair, knowing she hated that shit but I didn't care. Like I said, I was about to punish that ass. "Tell me you're sorry."

"I… Uhh… sorr…y." She couldn't get a full sentence out. I smacked her ass, "That's what I thought!"

I swear we went at it for hours. I threw her little ass in every position I could think of. By time we were done, we both fell on the bed, breathing hard as hell and sweaty as shit. "Damn," was all she could say.

I went up there with the intention of having a serious talk with her. *Fuck that, the shit can wait till another time.* I got up and reached for her hand. "Let's go take a shower and get some sleep."

"I can't move."

I laughed and picked her up and carried her to the bathroom. I turned the shower on and put her in it. We took our time washing each other. I really loved that girl and could see myself spending the rest of my life with her. Fuck her bitch ass baby daddy! He had his turn to do right by her, but he fucked it up. Now I was going to show him how it was done. I refused to end things with her, that was exactly what he wanted.

Reneice

I was on my way to Kamil's club to surprise him. I hadn't been there since the night of my birthday, so I decided to go show my baby some love. Of course, I had my right hand, Le'Lani, with me. Since I knew everyone that worked there and my baby was the boss, there was no standing in line for us.

"Hey Miss Lady," my favorite bouncer Timbo said. "Long time no see."

"I know right, I thought I would come out and bless y'all with my presence tonight," I joked as I walked in the club with Lani at my side.

While Lani headed to VIP to get us a table, I headed for the stairs to Kamil's office.

"Hey Neicey, umm, what you doing here?" Frog, another bouncer asked.

"What you not happy to see me?"

"Yeah, it's just I didn't know you were coming," he said looking at the stairs.

"Ya boy in his office?" I asked.

"Uhh, yeah he... he up there," he answered looking at the stairs once again.

I knew something was going on because he kept looking at those damn stairs. I walked past his big ass as if I was on a mission.

When I got to Kamil's office, I stood outside and heard voices. One of them belonged to a female. She was giggling like a damn church girl. I opened the door and saw that bitch sitting on Kamil's desk right in front of his ass. He was grinning from ear to ear like the damn joker.

"I really hope I'm not interrupting anything. I would hate to have to shoot this bitch up," I said in a deadly tone.

Kamil jumped up and walked towards me. "Uhh, hey baby, what are you doing here?"

I passed him and a bitch that had too much makeup caked on her face. She was wearing a smirk that was about 2 seconds from being slapped off.

"Dismiss yo bitch before I set it off in here, and on my momma's grave, I'm not playing," I said never taking my eyes off that hoe.

"It's time for you to go," Kamil said turning around.

"What you mean it's time for me to go? You weren't telling me to leave when I had your dick in my mouth," she said, rolling her neck.

I just rolled my eyes and reached in my purse. "Yo Neicey chill," Kamil said.

I ignored him, pulled a stack out, and slapped the bitch with it. "Now he asked you to leave, don't make him ask you again," I said.

She wasted no time picking up the money and leaving the office. I cut my eyes at Kamil. "I'll deal with yo stupid ass later," I said before leaving him in his office.

"Neicey," he called out, but I kept walking as if I didn't hear shit.

I went to find Lani in VIP, when I got there; Kamil's hoe and her friends were looking like they had something to say. I just looked at the busted hoes and went on about my business.

"Wassup mami? How ya boy doing?" Lani asked.

I shrugged and called for a waiter. *I need a drink and I need one now,* I thought as I ordered a bottle of 1800 Silver.

"Alright Niecey, talk to me. You just ordered some liquor and you don't even drink, that's not you, so wassup," Lani said, looking at me seriously.

"I'm cool boo, just got a lot on my mind. Let's hit the floor," I said getting up.

We made our way to the dance floor and of course, all eyes were on us. I had some liquor in my system and felt like acting an ass, so I grabbed the first nigga that I saw to dance with. The DJ was playing Chris Brown and Nicki Minaj's "Love More" so I was showing out, especially since those were two of my favorite artists.

I started grinding my ass on the stranger while he grabbed my hips. Shit, I knew that was Kamil's club and his ass was probably somewhere watching, but at the moment, I was feeling like fuck him. I was all into the music feeling the hell out of myself when all of a sudden I felt somebody grab my arm.

"What the fuck is wrong with you?" Kamil yelled.

"Kamil, calm down," Lani said coming over to us.

"Nigga leave me the fuck alone," I said snatching away from him.

"Yo, let's go, we're going home."

"Nah nigga, I didn't come with you, so I'm not leaving with you. You just worry about that bitch over there," I said pointing to the bitch that was in his office. "Lani, let's go."

Fuck him; he could do him while I did me. He must have forgotten that his ass could be replaced.

Kamil

No lie, I felt like shit. I didn't know Neicey was about to show her ass up at the club. Two days later, and she still wouldn't talk to me, so I was going shopping and preparing to do some ass kissing. I saw a cute ass tennis bracelet and necklace that I wanted get her at Tiffany's. I also decided to get some her some purple roses and a big ass teddy bear. I know, I was a sucka ass nigga, but a happy wife means a happy life.

I walked in the house looking for Neicey and I found her in the kitchen. Her back was facing me so I walked in and wrapped my arms around her.

"Fuck off Kamil," she said trying to move away from me.

I just picked her little ass up and sat her on the counter. "You still mad at me?" I asked standing between her legs.

She peeked around me and noticed the Tiffany's bag. "Maybe," she said.

"What I gotta do to make it up?" I asked rubbing her thigh.

"Hand me that bag."

"Oh so you just want the gifts huh? How I know you'll forgive me if I give you the bag?"

"It all depends what you got me."

"Okay, give me a kiss and I'll give it to you."

She looked at me sideways like I was crazy. "I don't know where yo lips been."

"The last time I checked they were down there," I said pointing to her crotch.

"I probably wasn't the only one," she said, rolling her neck.

"Get the fuck out of here man, all the bitch did was sick my dick. It ain't like I fucked her or nothing."

"And? That's still classified as cheating. If he wanted that shit, I would have stayed with Mykell."

I hated when she brought that nigga up. "If I can forgive you for fucking him, why you can't forgive me?"

She rolled her eyes. "Whatever."

"I thought so, now give me a kiss."

She finally gave in and gave me a kiss. "That's what I'm talking about, now was that so hard?" I laughed.

"Shut up and give me the bag."

I handed her the Tiffany's bag and she smiled from ear to ear when she saw what I'd gotten her.

I took the necklace and bracelet and put them on her. "You still love me?" I asked.

"Hmm, it's debatable." She laughed. "Hand me my flowers so I can put them in some water."

My job was done.

Chapter 8

Reneice

The past two weeks had been crazy! , I was meeting up with Le'Lani so she could help me with some wedding stuff. I didn't really know how that was going to work because Lani was the only female I messed with, so, of course, she would be the maid of honor, but I wouldn't have any bridesmaids. Kamil wasn't close to anybody that could be his best man and Ramone was definitely out of the question.

I walked into my brother's house like I lived there, shit, I might as well. "Keep walking in here like that and I'ma start collecting rent from yo ass."

"Whatever! Where ya girl at?"

"Right here," Lani said coming down the stairs.

I sat on the couch, "Alright boo, let's get down to business."

"Oh I gotta stick around for this one," Ramone smirked.

I just flipped him the bird.

"You know what colors you want?" Lani asked.

"Of course purple and white."

"I should've known."

"Do you have a date yet?"

"I'm thinking sometime in August."

"Who's walking you down the aisle?" Ramone asked.

"Uh, you right?" I asked confused.

"I think you better call Dad up for this one or ask Pops because you already know I don't approve of this shit, so I'm still contemplating if I even wanna show up."

My jaw hit the floor at the shit he was talking. "Are you serious Ramone?"

"Serious as hell. You already know I don't rock with that nigga at all. Honestly, I think you will be making a big ass mistake if you go through with this. I'm your brother so you know I'm not gonna lie to you."

"Ramone," Lani yelled.

"What?"

"Was that really necessary?" she fussed.

"It's cool Lani, whether you know it or not my brother's opinion means a lot to me. It's just crazy that he feels so strongly about it that he wouldn't even show up. I understand you not giving me away but you not showing up don't sit well with me."

"Ladybug, I've known you all your life. I pretty much know you better than you know yourself; I have a parental instinct I developed when I took you in. I know when someone isn't right for you when I look at them. I'm telling you that he is not the one."

"Why you never said anything before then Ramone," I sighed

"Because you're grown and I was never one to interfere in your relationships unless I felt some shit wasn't right. Well, I've never felt that way until you got with this nigga. I thought it was just a phase you were going through and you would get over him soon. Now you're talking about marrying this nigga. So I have no choice but to step in and do my job."

"Ramone, I'm pretty sure she can take care of herself. She wouldn't be going through all this if she didn't want to be with him. So why wait until they get this far to break them up?" Lani asked.

"Because that's my sister, my baby sister, my only sister. I refuse to sit back and let her make the biggest mistake of her life. I get a funny vibe from this nigga, something about him ain't right, and I'll be damned if I let him get my Ladybug into some shit. Just like Micah and Mykell would do the same for you."

"Are you sure this has nothing to do with him pulling that gun out on you?" I asked trying to see where my brother's head was.

"Come on now Reneice." *He used my government name so he must be serious.* "You know me; I've been in the streets since I was a little nigga. I know how to analyze people and when I say I know a nigga ain't right, ten times out of ten, he ain't right."

I just sat back taking in everything my brother said. He was right, whenever he felt some way about somebody he always seemed to be right. Now I was confused about what to do. "Look, mami, I know that's your brother and you care about his opinion but you need to do whatever makes *you* happy. Not anyone else," Lani said.

"Shut up Le'Lani!"

"Ramone Tyshaun Peake, go find you some business," she fussed at him.

"Last time I checked my sister was my business."

"Okay you guys, that's enough. I have to go pick up my son from his father's house then I have to go home and get dinner started. I'll talk to you two later."

* * *

Kamil was out of town handling business, so it was just my Fat Man and me. I fixed us some breakfast then put him in my bed and turned on some cartoons for him while I jumped in the shower. My mind was all over the place. I was thinking about what Ramone said. I was a little hurt that he wouldn't come to the wedding if I went through with it. He was feeling some type of way about Kamil and that bothered me. *Could Kamil really be no good for me? Was I making the biggest mistake of my life? Was I going to regret this in the end?*

My thoughts were interrupted when I heard Romell laughing. *He must really be into those cartoons.* I wrapped my towel around me and walked out of the bathroom. I damn near jumped out of my skin when I saw who was lying in the bed as if they belonged here.

"Oh my God! What the fuck are you doing here?" I said as my towel dropped. I hadn't seen Mykell since Romell's birthday, and I really didn't want to see him then. I had no words for his black ass.

I bent down to pick my towel up. "What you rushing to cover up for? You're acting like I ain't never seen that ass naked before," he smirked. "But to answer your question, I came to spend time with my son. Especially since you haven't let me see him in three weeks."

I went to my drawer, putting my panties and bra on, ignoring everything he was saying. "How did you get in my house Mykell?"

"That doesn't matter."

"Ugh! Can you get out so I can finish getting dressed?" I asked becoming irritated.

"Girl, gon' head with that bullshit!"

I threw on some leggings and a t-shirt. I grabbed Romell out of the bed and walked downstairs. I couldn't be in the room with him because I didn't know what he would try.

"Where's MJ?"

"Spending time with his new mom." I knew he was just saying that shit to get a rise out of me but I wasn't about to play games with him.

"Why are you here?"

"I already told you, I'm here for my son. I also wanna see what that booty do," he laughed after hitting me on my ass.

I rolled my eyes, "Well your son is right here, but you will *never* be able to taste this again."

"Is that right?" he asked walking closer to me. "Never say never. I'm like Ray J, I hit it first," he laughed.

I just shook my head. "Mykell don't play with me. You said you wanted your son, so get him, if not, leave. You shouldn't be here anyways."

"Says who?"

"Says me. Last time I checked your name wasn't on shit in this house."

"Except yo ass. Now stop playing and come here."

"Mykell, don't make me slap you," I laughed at that fool.

"Aight man," he said, picking Romell up.

"Man, yo mama acting all funny and shit. Now that the cat out of the bag, she act like she don't want it no more. Everybody already knows. We might as well keep it going. We might even make you a little sister."

I walked over to him and hit him in the head. "Why you always gotta talk shit?"

"I thought you liked it when I talk shit," he said, winking.

"Ugh, I can't stand you."

"I love you too."

"Whatever."

Conceited ass.

Kya

Kya: I heard my cousin is out of town so she and the little bastards should be there by themselves right now.

Unknown: Perfect.

I was happy that it was finally happening just so I could be done with it. I had been trying for the longest to get rid of that bitch, but it was as if she refused to go anywhere. Well, she had no choice that day. *R.I.P.* I thought to myself.

Chapter 9

Mykell

"I don't know why yo ass always gotta act funny." I was getting tired of going through the motions with her ass.

"I'm not acting funny, you said you wanted your son, well get him. Any other bullshit you came for is dead! Never again."

"Fuck out..."

TAT! TAT! POP! BOOM!

I was cut short by the sound of guns and bullets ripping through the house.

"Ahhh! Romell," I heard Neicey scream.

At that moment, I didn't give a fuck about being hit. I was more worried about protecting my family.

I grabbed Romell off the couch, then ran over to Neicey and pushed her to the ground, using my body to protect them both. Only God knew I wouldn't be able to live with myself if I lost either one of them,

TATTTT-BOOM!

It sounded like cannons. My lil man was screaming his heart out and Neicey was shaking. We stayed that way until I didn't hear any more gunshots. When it got quiet, I immediately checked my son to make sure he wasn't hit. He was fine, just a little shook up. Neicey was okay too, and that was all that mattered to me.

"Let's get the fuck out of here before they come back."

"What if they're still outside?"

"I'll check. You stay here."

I ran to the window and peeked out. I didn't see any cars or anything suspicious. I wasn't one to take any chances, so I checked to make sure I had my pistol on me. I looked over at Neicey and she was trying to comfort Romell and calm him down. "It's okay Fat Man, Mama's got her baby."

"Yo, you still got that thing, Ma?" I asked, referring to her gun.

"I never leave home without it."

Gangsta ass, I thought to myself.

"Aight, come on. Let's get the fuck out of here."

Neicey rode in the back with Romell because he was still crying his eyes out; eventually she got him to fall asleep. She pulled out her phone and called somebody.

"Where are you?"

I looked at her in the rearview mirror and could tell she was pissed from her facial expressions.

"Somebody shot up the damn house while me and my son were in it!"

"We'll talk about it later." She hung up.

She put her head back on the seat and I could see the tears running down her face. I was about to get to the bottom of that shit. Something could have happened to my babies and I would have had to fuck the city up!

I pulled up in Pops' driveway. Neicey got out with Romell in her arms and walked in the house. She went straight upstairs, to lay down, I assumed. "What's wrong with Mommy? Why's she crying?" MJ was on it, never missing a beat.

"She's fine lil man. Where's your grandpa?"

"Right here," Pops said walking out of the kitchen.

"We've got major issues, Pops," I sighed.

"What's wrong?"

"I went to go get Romell to spend some time with him, but when I got there muthafuckas got to shooting up the damn house. My damn girl and son were in there, I could have lost them."

Pops didn't say anything. He just shook his head and walked to his office. He did that when shit got real and he had to make some phone calls and handle some business. I took that as an opportunity to go check on Neicey and Romell. I found them laying down in my old room. I went and sat on the bed by Neicey. I rubbed her hair, and she just looked at me.

"You know I'ma get to the bottom of this shit right?"

She shook her head, "No Kell, I don't want you out there getting hurt or getting locked back up."

"Gon' head girl, what kind of man would I be if I let somebody get away with trying to hurt my family?"

"Do you think they were after me or Kamil?"

"You ain't beefing with nobody are you?"

"No, especially not anybody that would want me dead."

"Then I'm pretty sure they were after ya boy."

"Knock, knock." I turned around to see Pops. "I made some calls and everybody has their ears to the streets. We're going to handle this. Where's Kamil?"

"He's in Atlanta handling business."

"Okay, well y'all are staying here until he gets back."

"I'ma stay here with them."

"You don't have to," Neicey tried to protest, but I shut that shit down.

"You heard what I said. Now get some rest."

Some foul shit going on here, I can feel it.

Ramone

I got off the phone with Mykell and my heart damn near dropped to my stomach. Too much shit was happening to my sister and it was funny how her so-called nigga wasn't ever around when shit went down. He was suspect in my eyes and he was guilty until proven innocent. I had to call my boys and let them know it was time to get down and dirty like we used to. I had their asses on standby until it was time to handle that shit. Mykell said he wanted to do some research before we handled it so that was what we were going to do. Don't nobody mess with my family and get away with it. I decided to call Dad and let him know what was up.

"Hello?"

"Dad somebody shot up Ladybug's house while she and Romell were there."

"What the fuck! Are they okay?"

"Yeah they made it out untouched. Pops has them staying with him until her nigga gets back in town."

"Where the fuck was he at? Matter of fact, never mind. I'm on my way."

I looked at the phone and he hung up before I could even respond.

"What's wrong?" Lani asked walking into the room.

"Somebody shot up the Neicey's house."

"Oh my God! Is she okay?"

"Yeah, Romell was a little shook up, but Mykell was there with them when it happened and he took em to Pop's house."

"We gotta go see her!"

"Pops said to let them get some rest and come see them tomorrow."

"Where the hell was Kamil?"

"Good ass question, he's supposedly out of town handling business."

"Yeah right."

I knew I wasn't the only one that was feeling some type of way about that nigga.

Kya

Kya: You fucked up, Mykell was in that house with them, and nobody got hurt.

Unknown: That just means we have to up our guns and come a little harder. No worries, it will be handled.

Kya: How do you plan on doing that?

Unknown: Watch and learn.

I had a feeling that the shit was going to come back and bite me in the ass.

Chapter 10

Reneice

It had been a week and Kamil's ass still wasn't home. You would think that the moment I told him the house was shot up; he would've been on the first thing smoking back home. But nope, that nigga still had his bright ass in Atlanta. Talking about he couldn't leave until he was finished handling his business. Fuck him and that business! Even my dad came to see me. He'd been there ever since he found out what happened and refused to leave until he got some answers. *What the fuck is really going on? Who would want me dead?*

"Wassup, Knucklehead?"

My thoughts were broken by Micah. "Nothing much Mack, just racking my brain trying to figure this shit out."

"Don't even stress it. You just worry about taking care of my nephew and let us big dogs worry about that other shit."

"It's kind of hard doing that when I'm a damn walking target and I don't know who's gunning for my head," I fumed.

I looked at Micah and he was looking at me as if I was crazy.

"I'm sorry Mack, I didn't mean to take it out on you, but this is really stressing me out. I have to watch my back now every time I leave the house."

"It's cool baby sis, I understand, but you know good and damn well we're not gonna let nothing happen to you. Kell, Mone, and I may be out of the game now, but that don't mean that shit ain't in us no more. We don't have no problem busting our guns for yo lil ass." He mushed me.

I just laughed. "Now that's what I'm talking about. I've been looking for that smile for the longest," he said.

"Yeah, if she don't keep smiling I'ma end up kicking her ass," Mykell said, walking in the room.

"Where you been?" I asked.

"Wouldn't you like to know?"

"No never mind, you're grown. Do you."

Ever since the shooting, I looked at Mykell in a different way. He could have said to hell with me and just worried about his son. Instead, he looked out for both of us and that really meant a lot to me. He had been helping me and staying there with us, not once had he made a pass at me or tried to sleep with me.

"Wassup, Mackaroni, where you been?" he spoke to his brother.

"Took a little vacation, and now I'm back and ready to handle business."

"Good, that's what I like to hear."

"Umm, where's Romell and MJ?" I interrupted their conversation.

"Downstairs chilling with their grandpas," Mykell answered. He was about to say something else when his phone started to ring. He looked at his phone and smiled. "Excuse me guys, but I need to get this."

I cut my eyes at him wondering who was calling him that had him grinning like a damn cheetah cat. *Why does it even matter, we're not together anyways.*

"So y'all back on track or something?"

"Absolutely, not! He has his hoes and I have Kamil." I said.

"Unh huh. So where is Kamil now?"

"Atlanta."

"Does he know what happened?"

"Yeah, but he said he can't leave until he finishes handling business."

He looked at me as if I was crazy. He started to say something but I cut him off.

"I know, I know. Just leave it be until he gets here."

"Alright, but let's go see my nephews."

We made our way downstairs where I saw my Fat Man chilling in my dad's lap.

"Aww, look at my four favorite men chilling together."

"Hey Ladybug," my dad spoke.

"Hey Dad, hey Pop-Pop."

"Wassup baby girl?"

"You two are too hip for me," I chuckled.

"You know I'm far from old. I'm only 46. Now that man over there," he pointed to my dad. "He's old," he said and laughed.

"Yeah right. I'm only 46 too. So if I'm old, what does that make you?"

"I'm happy to see you two are getting close," I said sitting next to Pop-Pop.

"Girl, see what I didn't tell you is, we actually know each other. How do you think I knew where to find you?" my dad asked.

"What? How do you know each other?" I asked confused.

"His wife's brother and I used to be best friends."

"Ms. Cherry?"

"Yup! I knew Mykell and Micah when they were little snotty nose kids. They moved here before Le'Lani was born so I didn't know about her," my dad explained.

"This is too much. Did you know that when you took me in Pop-Pop?"

"I didn't until after I had a conversation with Mone. That was after the little incident we had downstairs and I had to beat his ass."

"Wow!"

"I know right."

Mykell

I didn't miss that look Neicey gave me before I walked out of the room. I knew she still loved a nigga and after the shit I just found out, her ass would be home where she belonged. I had to call Mone so I could share that information with my brothers.

"Yo Mone, get ya ass here nigga. I've got some shit I know you would love to hear."

"I'm already in route bruh."

"Good."

I went downstairs to get Mack. "Yo Micah, let me holla at you." He knew I was serious because I used his government.

"What y'all need to talk about?" Neicey asked.

"I'll let you know later."

"Ugh whatever," she said and rolled her eyes.

I'll deal with her ass later.

"What's the problem?" Mack asked as soon as we made it to the basement.

"Man, I just found out some crazy shit. I'm just waiting for Mone to get here so I can get it out of my system."

"Well, don't keep an asshole in suspense, let me know wassup," Ramone said, walking down the stairs.

"Damn nigga, what you do? Speed here?" I asked

"I told you I was already in route. Now spill it."

"So I had somebody do some investigation for me. Well come to find out, Kamil went to Kya's house the day he left."

"Okay, well you already knew he was going over there from that one day we saw him coming out," Micah said.

"If you would let me finish. Anyways, he's not really in Atlanta he's in Cali, which is where he's originally from. He's a contract killer! Now this shit is too much of a coincidence for me."

"What the fuck! How did you find all this out?" Ramone asked

"C'mon now, you really think I'ma have a nigga around my family and I don't do some research on his ass? Yeah, it took me longer than it should have, but I got it done."

"So what does all this have to do with Kya? You think she hired him to kill baby girl?" Micah inquired.

"Nah, I don't think she's got enough heart to pull some shit like this off."

"Fuck that," Ramone said. "Ladybug! Come here!"

"Man you can't tell her yet," I said

"Tell me what?" she said coming down the stairs

"Did you know that Kamil and Kya know each other?" Micah asked her.

"Yeah, they're cousins."

I looked at her then at my brothers.

Her phone started ringing before anybody could say anything else.

"Hello?"

"Okay, I'll meet you there. I'm on my way right now."

She looked at us, "Okay I'll get up with y'all later. My man is home and wants me to come see him."

I looked at Micah and Ramone; they already knew what I was thinking.

"Y'all keep an eye on MJ and Mell. I'm following her because I don't trust this nigga."

"We're rolling with you," Ramone said.

"Naw bruh, I'ma do this one by myself."

Chapter 11

Reneice

I was a little confused about Kamil wanting me to meet him at the old house. *Why the fuck would he want me to meet him at a house that's boarded up?*

Well, I got my answer when I pulled up and saw the house looked as good as new. I was shocked. I got out of the car and walked right on in.

"How do you like it?" Kamil asked with a big smile on his face.

"Oh my God! When did you do this?"

"Did you really think I wasn't going to bring my ass home when I heard about what happened? Naw baby, that ain't even me."

"How did you do this though?" I asked looking around at the newly remodeled house.

"Ya man got connects baby," he boasted.

"I love it Kamil, I really do, but I don't feel safe staying here after what happened."

"I knew you were going to say that. Actually, I was going to put this house up for sale and we hoping you would move to California with me. We can get married out there and be a happy family. Just you, me, and Romell."

"I don't think that shit is about to happen," I heard from behind me. I turned around to see Mykell standing there.

"Mykell what are you doing here?"

"I came to let you know that this nigga ain't really who you think he is."

"What are you talking about?" I asked irritated.

"Nigga you just don't give up do you? You're that mad I got her that you would come up in here on some bullshit? You need to suck this shit up and leave us alone because whether you like it or not, we're going to be together and we are going to get married."

"We'll see about that after she finds out what you really do," Mykell smirked.

"Alright enough of this bullshit! What the fuck is going on?" I was starting to get mad as hell. Everybody wanted to talk in riddles instead of keeping shit real.

"Apparently you don't know who you're sleeping with," Kya said walking from the back of the house.

I looked at Kamil with a look of death. "You had this bitch in my house? Really?"

"Baby, I didn't know she was here," he turned to Kya. "What the fuck are you doing here Rahkya?"

"I just came to see how my favorite cousin was after his trip to Cali," she smirked.

"What the fuck she mean Cali, I thought you were in Atlanta?"

"Naw, baby. Ya man over here was in Cali, that's where he's from. Supposedly he's a contract killer," Mykell said.

"What the fuck is he talking about Kamil?" I asked, wondering what was really going on.

He didn't answer; instead, he pulled his gun out and pointed it at Mykell. He was a little too late because Mykell already had his out.

"Nigga say another fucking word and I'll kill you right where you stand," Kamil threatened.

"Whatever fuck boy, if you were really bout it, you would have been done it instead of talking."

I walked in the middle of them because nobody was about to die until I got some answers. "I'm not going to ask no more. What the fuck is going on?" I asked through gritted teeth.

"Oh wait. I have somebody that can answer that question," Kya smirked and answered.

In walked some light-skinned trick with a smile on her face like some shit was funny.

Mykell

I was shocked as hell when I saw Olivia walk through the door. I hadn't seen her since she gave birth to MJ. *How the fuck did these two bitches hookup together.* "Remember me?" she smirked.

The last time I saw Olivia was before I got locked up. It had been a while since I saw the mother of my first-born. She was still as beautiful as ever with her peanut butter complexion, light brown eyes and banging body, but she didn't have shit on Neicey. Olivia and I messed around for about a year before she got pregnant with MJ. To this day, I still don't know how the hell that happened because I always made sure I strapped up.

She was one of my favorite side bitches because she always kept her mouth shut and played her position, but all that changed when she found out she was pregnant. She thought that gave her the right to be wifey but she thought wrong. After I was locked up, I found out that she was doing drugs around my son and was sleeping with random niggas for money. That shit wasn't flying with me, so I had my dad go get my son and he had been away from her ass ever since.

"Who the fuck is this Mykell?" Neicey asked.

I didn't even know how to tell her.

"I'm his *first* baby mama," she replied with an attitude.

"Huh?" Kya spoke.

I still had my gun pointed at Kamil, but I was focused on Kya and Olivia. "Yes bitch. I'm Mykell Junior's real mother. Not this wanna be."

"You didn't tell me that," Kya said.

"I didn't have to."

"So you're just doing dirty work for bitches and don't know nothing about em? Fuck type of shit you on Rahkya," I yelled.

"So from the moment you approached me, you knew who I was?" Kya asked. She turned and looked at me. "So this is the bitch you cheated on me with and had a baby by?"

"Man, Kya that shit happened eight damn years ago," I fumed.

"Fuck them bitches! Both of em, you were supposed to be mine. You fucked around on me and made a baby with this bitch," she pointed at Olivia. "Then came home and had a baby with that other bitch," she pointed at Neicey.

Neicey pulled her gun from behind her and shot Kya in the head so fast that if I wasn't looking, I probably would have missed it. Kamil had a gun pointed at me, I had one pointed at him, Neicey had hers pointed at Olivia, and Olivia had hers pointed at me. *This shit is crazy.* "Kamil, why did you turn weak on me?" Olivia asked.

"What is she talking about Kamil?" Neicey asked with a look of death in her eyes.

"Tell her Kamil," Olivia taunted.

He just stood there looking at me. "Well, since you won't talk, I will. Well little girl, your fiancé here was supposed to get rid of your ass. But he got weak and fell in love with you, why I don't know. I paid him to do a job that he failed to do," Olivia explained with an evil look.

"Really Kamil? So you did have something to do with the house getting shot up? You had something to do with me being raped and MJ being taken? My son was in that fucking house!" Neicey was on the verge of tears and I was ready to put a bullet right in the middle of his forehead.

"Baby look, I didn't know she wanted you raped. She just wanted you to be roughed up a little, but I backed out at the last minute. As for MJ being taken, I really didn't have shit to do with that. I swear I didn't know her ass was going to shoot up the house or else I never would have left y'all here. I haven't communicated with her or Kya in months!"

"This nigga lying Neicey, he was just at Kya's house the other day! That's why I asked you if you knew they were cool," I butted in.

Olivia just laughed. "You find something funny with the fact that you had another woman beaten and raped? Then you laugh because your son was kidnapped? Had somebody's house shot up? Bitch, my son was in that fucking house when you did that shit!" I was ready to kill both those bitches.

"Oh silly you, MJ wasn't kidnapped. I had him the whole time. You must be crazy as hell to think that I would hurt my own child. I just wanted to keep him away from this bitch. As for that bastard y'all share together, I don't give a fuck about him. You had my baby taken away from me when he was only six months old! Then you get with her ass and have her raising my son. *My son,* Mykell."

"This bitch, as you call her was the one that took in your son, loved him, cared for him, spent time with him, raised him when yo trifling ass couldn't. He knows her as his mom, not you bitch," I had to set her ass straight.

"So it's my fault Mykell?"

"Who else's fault was it?"

"It was yours! I had yo fucking child but you acted like I ain't mean shit to you. Then you had yo dad come and take him from me."

"Yeah, because yo ass chose drugs and niggas over yo son. Don't fucking act like you care about him now," I yelled, getting pissed at that dumb ass bitch.

"Man, fuck all this shit. I have two sons that are waiting for their mommy to come get them. So if we could just hurry up with this bullshit," Neicey said ready to put a bullet in Olivia.

"I have one question Olivia, how the hell did y'all link up?"

She chuckled and shook her head. "You know it's funny that I always knew who Kya was, but she never knew who I was. All I did was approach her one day acting like I liked her shoes. I wanted to know if you two were still together. She informed that you had a new bitch in the picture and how she wanted her ass gone. I acted like I had a personal vendetta against Neicey too just to see how serious she was about having her gone. She mentioned she had a cousin that lived in Cali that kills people for a living and I just knew I hit the jackpot. The plan was to get rid of this bitch then eventually get rid of Kya so we could be a family like we're supposed to be."

Neicey laughed. "Mykell you sure do like them psycho, deranged ass bitches don't you?"

"Bitch nobody asked you shit," she yelled at Neicey. She then turned and smiled at me devilishly.

"Kamil, off him," she ordered, and then she turned to Neicey.

Everything happened so fast that I didn't have time to react. I heard Neicey scream, "No," then I heard gunshots. After that, everything turned black.

Chapter 12

Mykell

I can see the light, I reached out to try and grab it. "Baby you don't want to do that."

"Mama?"

"Yes, baby. I wouldn't go to it if I were you, I don't think it's a good idea."

She still looked as beautiful as the last time I saw her. She was carrying a baby in her arms but it was wrapped up.

"Who is that Mama? And why can't I go to the light?"

"This is your son…"

"My son?"

"Yes, I'm watching over the baby you and Reneice lost. But to answer your question, you can't go to the light because you have a family that would miss you. You have to finish watching over MJ and Romell. What would they do without their daddy?" she smiled sweetly.

"No Mama, I wanna stay here with you and my son. You left me when I was a little boy. You never got to see me grow up."

"Oh baby, I've been up here watching over you, Micah, Le'Lani, and your dad the whole time. I'm proud of you guys. But I can't allow you to stay here with us."

"But I don't want to be down there anymore. I want to stay here with you guys," I pleaded.

"Now, Mykell. You heard what I said, you have a family down there that needs you much more, then we need you right now. It's not your time, when we're ready for you we'll come get you."

"Can I hold him?"

"Sure."

I took him into my arms and he looked just like his mom. He even has her dimples. "Hey little man, you look just like your mom."

"He's handsome. Just like my other two grandsons."

"He is handsome huh?"

"Yes, now you need to go back down there and give me a beautiful little granddaughter."

"Okay, I'll try."

"Don't try, just do it."

"Okay Mama, I love you."

"I love you too, baby, we'll be here waiting for you, but don't come back anytime soon."

"Okay."

"Alright, we got him. He's back," I heard someone yell.

*   *   *

I opened my eyes and looked around. I didn't know where I was. I heard a beeping noise and tried to sit up. What the hell did I do that for? I had pain shoot through my chest when I did that.

"He's awake," I heard someone say.

Lani came over to my bed and lifted it up.

"Push the button to get the nurse," I heard my pops say.

Two minutes later, a nurse walked in the room. "Nice to see you up Mr. Jones."

"How long have I been here?" I asked suddenly remembering what happened to get me there.

"Just a couple of hours," she responded checking my vitals.

After she was done, she left the room. As soon as she left, Micah came and sat on my bed. "Man don't ever scare us like that again. We thought we had lost you."

"You know I'm too stubborn to go anywhere man. I have two sons that need me, so I can't go nowhere. But how did I get here?"

"We called the ambulance after we walked in the house. You should've known I wasn't about to let my little brother go in there by himself. While you were following baby girl, we were following you."

"That's love man. That shit was crazy though, it was something straight out of a soap opera."

"You can tell me about it later."

I looked over and saw Romell asleep in Pop's arms. "Come here MJ."

He came over looking sad like he had been crying. "Wassup man, I'm straight, quit crying. Daddy ain't going nowhere."

He hugged my neck and I felt that pain shoot through my chest again.

"Arghh!"

"Okay little man, let Daddy get some rest," Micah said.

Ramone had a far-off look in his eyes. *What the fuck is wrong with him?* I looked around the room and noticed everybody was looking that way and like they had been crying. Even Neicey's dad had tears in his eyes. *Speaking of, where she got her ass at?* I thought to myself.

"Aye, man, where's Neicey at?" I asked my brother.

Ramone rushed out of the room when I asked that question and of course, Lani ran after him. Nobody answered my question.

"Let me guess, she had to go identify that nigga's body? It's cool; she'll probably come see me later."

"What do you mean identify his body?" Micah asked looking confused.

"I know I shot that nigga and he's dead. So she probably had to identify his body since Kya can't do it."

"Bruh there was only three bodies when we got there."

"Yeah. Kya, Kamil, and me. So Olivia got away huh?"

"No, you, Kya and Neicey. What do you mean Olivia got away?"

"Wait, what do you mean Neicey was one of the bodies there? Where is she?"

"First, tell me what you mean Olivia by was there?"

"Olivia was the one who hired Kamil to get rid of Neicey. Now once again where is Reneice?" I asked sternly.

"Umm," he held his head down.

"Come on man. Don't do this to me. She not gone man, she can't be. She has to be here to watch Romell grow and make sure MJ do right. She not gone."

I had tears streaming down my face but I didn't give a fuck. That was the first time I'd cried in forever and I deserved to. My heart was gone. I felt like less of a man because I didn't protect her.

Ramone

"It's okay baby, just let it go," Lani said while rubbing my back. I hadn't cried since I lost my mama but that shit was eating me up. I had failed my sister. I wasn't there to protect her like I promised her I would. *What kind of brother am I?*

"It's my fault Lani, I failed her. I let that bitch take my sister away from me. The sad thing about it is his ass is still out there breathing."

"Shhh, it is not your fault. This was all his fault. You told her how you felt, and you were right, he just got to her before she could leave. Don't worry he's going to get his."

"I gotta call my boys," I said taking my phone out of my pocket.

"Yo Mone wassup?" Corey answered.

"She's gone man," I said barely above a whisper.

"What? Speak up man I can't hear you!"

"She's gone."

"Who?"

I cried.

"Man don't say that. Are you serious? Know what, say no more. We on our way."

I hung up and saw my dad coming towards us.

"Did you tell him?" I asked

"Yeah, he's not taking it too good."

"Shit, none of us are. I just called Corey and them so they know. They said they're on the way up here. I already know this shit is gonna kill Lakey."

My phone started ringing. *Speaking of the devil.*

"Yo," my voice cracked.

"Man tell me this shit ain't true Mone. Tell me you playing; tell me my Snook ain't gone." I could tell he was crying.

"I wish I could man."

"Y'all got that nigga right?"

"He got away."

"FUCK THAT! THAT BITCH GOTTA GO," he yelled before he hung up.

Kamil

I didn't mean to shoot her. She jumped in the way and was shot. That bitch nigga shot me in my shoulder and that shit burned like hell. If he wouldn't have run his mouth and just left us alone, none of that would have happened. It was all his fault. I went to see one of my old friends and he patched my ass up. Now all I had to do was hop on my private jet and I was gone. I'd be on my way back to Cali.

I really did hate that the shit happened. I really did love her. If I didn't, I would have just offed her ass and collected my money. What nigga you know would turn down some money for a female if he wasn't really feeling her? I admit, in the beginning, I was doing my job then I fell for her little ass.

I knew I got that nigga because I put a couple more in his chest, so I didn't have to worry about him coming after me.

Ramone

Lani started to breakdown. She had been so strong, but I could tell she had finally reached her breaking point.

I took her into my arms. "It's okay Ma, she's in a better place. She's up there watching over us and laughing because we're down here doing all this crying,"

I said. I could just imagine her up there laughing and talking shit because everybody was down here crying. Especially me, she was probably up there calling me a little bitch and clowning me.

"I want her down here. What am I supposed to do without my best friend, hell, my only friend?" Lani cried.

"Shhh, she'll always be in our hearts. You know we'll never forget her little feisty self."

"What about MJ and Romell? They need their mother. I know Romell is too young to understand right now, but this is going to stick with MJ."

"They have us Ma. They'll be fine."

"I didn't even get to tell her I'm pregnant." She cried some more.

I was about to say something before I saw the doctors rushing into Mykell's room. *What the fuck is wrong now?*

Chapter 13

Mykell

I couldn't believe it. I refused to believe it. She couldn't be gone, nah, she was not gone. Just the thought of her being gone had me losing it. My bullet wounds didn't compare to the pain I was feeling in my heart. Doctors and nurses came running in the room. I remembered the first time I laid eyes on her the day I came home from prison. I knew then I had to have her. Her smile, her laugh, the certain faces she would make, just everything about her seemed so perfect and now she was gone.

What was I supposed to tell our sons when they asked about her? Especially Romell, he was too little too understand that shit. She would never get to see him grow up and be a man. It just couldn't be real.

I was supposed to make her my wife. We were supposed to spend the rest of our lives together. Yeah, I messed with a couple of females here and there, but I knew Neicey was the one I wanted to spend the rest of my life with. I still had the ring I gave to her when I proposed. What nigga you know would go get a damn tattoo of a female's name if he didn't love her or plan to be with her forever. I remembered the first time I told her I loved her.

We were running around the house like two big ass kids. She was trying to run away from me because I kept tickling her.

"Mykell why you gotta play so much," she said, throwing one of the couch pillows at me.

"See, that's why you in trouble now," I said as I launched towards her. *She tried to run but I was too fast for her. I grabbed her, threw her on the couch, and started tickling her.*

"Kell, stoooooop! You about to make me pee on myself," she laughed uncontrollably.

"You done playing now?"

"Yessssss let me go," she laughed with tears in her eyes.

"Alright, I'm done. I don't want the baby to cry," I said letting her up.

"Asshole," she said.

"I love you too," I said getting up.

"You what?" she said giving me the side eye.

"I love you girl."

She looked like she was shocked. *"You shouldn't say things you don't mean,"* she fussed.

"I never do."

"So you love me?" she asked.

"Yes, I, Mykell, love you, Reneice."

That was one day of many that I will never forget. She was always so happy and always smiling. Now all that was gone and I had nothing but memories.

Kamil

I kept trying to wrap my mind around the fact that I actually shot the woman I loved. I knew she was going to be alright because her ass was too stubborn to die. I'd just give her a little time for things to cool off. Those bullets weren't meant for her, they were meant for that bitch ass Mykell, but before I knew what was happening she jumped in front of him.

I knew fucking with Rhakya's ass would get me into some shit. She was always getting somebody into something. She had been doing that since we were little. She would always do some conniving shit then I would have to go save her ass. I was really fucking happy she was dead. That made my life so much easier.

Ramone

I kept looking through my phone at all the crazy pictures I had of Neicey. She was always doing something to be the center of attention. I laughed when I came to a picture of her and Lani. They were like two peas in a pod. I remembered the day I made the promise to her that I would do anything to protect her.

It was the night after our mom's funeral. I was up because I couldn't sleep when I heard Neicey scream.

I ran to her room to find her breathing hard and sweating.

"What's wrong, Ladybug?" I asked.

"I'm scared," she said just above a whisper.

"Scared of what?"

"I don't know, I just feel like somebody is coming to get me and take me where mommy is," she said crying.

I took her into my arms and rocked her. "Ladybug, listen to me. As long as I have breath is my body, I will never let anything happen to you, or anybody hurt you. I'm here to protect you."

"You promise?" she asked.

"I promise."

I stayed in there with her until she fell asleep.

Now I felt like I failed her. I promised her that I would protect her and I couldn't even do that. I knew I should have put a bullet in that nigga's head a long ass time ago. I told her to leave him alone but I thought I was doing the right thing by letting her make her own decisions. The one time I should have put my foot down; I didn't and look what happened.

I looked up when I heard Lani coming towards me. Even through a crisis, she still was the most beautiful person I'd ever seen besides my sister and my mother.

"How's he holding up?"

"He's not. He's going crazy and cussing everybody out," she said.

"I'll go in and check on him in a minute, I just can't look at him right now."

She got quiet. "You know this isn't your fault. I know you feel like you were supposed to protect her, but nobody knew this was going to happen."

"Lani, what type of man am I when I can't even protect my family?" I asked.

"You're a great man that would do *anything* to protect his family. This was out of your control."

I just laid my head in her lap. I was so lucky to have a good woman on my side. She was so caring and understanding. She knew just what to say and when to say it. I didn't know what I would do without her.

Made in the USA
Lexington, KY
15 April 2016